DEATH DUEL

The way things happen in battle are seldom planned and I certainly didn't plan to have to fight off a dozen or more Comanches. That I managed to come out with most of them dead and the others hurtin' and the Indian attack completely routed was purely my good fortune and none of their own. I became a sort of token of bad medicine to the whole tribe. They set out to get rid of me in any handy way, and the handiest way was to set the Other One on me. That's the only name I had for him, and I ain't even sure where I picked it up. There wasn't much he wanted out of life except my scalp!

The Other One held all the high cards. He would pick the time and the place. If I took his challenge, I would probably die. Holdin' back never entered my mind. But I would do it my way. Not his.

Also by Dale Oldham:

TATE
BADLANDS DRIFTER

THE
SUDDEN
LAND

Dale Oldham

LEISURE BOOKS æ **NEW YORK CITY**

A LEISURE BOOK

Published by

Dorchester Publishing Co., Inc.
6 East 39th Street
New York, NY 10016

Printed in the United States of America

THE
SUDDEN
LAND

1

Annie Baxter

I licked my thumb and wiped it across the front sight of my squirrel rifle. The long, thin barrel was hot from the repeated charge and fire, charge and fire, charge. . . I wiped the sweat from my forehead on my sleeve. The Texas sun burned down. Oppressive, humid, heat held the stench of black powder smoke close to the ground. It burned every man's eyes and choked at our lungs. By that time, the boom of the heavy buffalo rifles on both sides of me had me half deaf. "Just what you deserve for tryin' to show off," I told myself.

The whole thing started because of the girl. If she hadn't been lookin' at me like that. . . You know how they do. With backs half turned and lookin' over their shoulder and pretendin' to be lookin' at something else. And all the while you know and they know that you know they're lookin' at you. Anyway, she was watchin' me like that. I tried to catch her eye, but she had played the game too often and managed to keep me a turn of the head behind. Well, I had played some myself. As innocent-seeming as I could, I took the Preacher's squirrel rifle out of my saddle sleeve and made a big show of checkin' it over from end to end. The shootin' match was about to start, and I wanted her to know I was one to contend with. I was as excited as a schoolboy the first time he notices the difference between the guys in britches and the ones in dresses. But I didn't jump around actin' silly. I ignored her completely while I made ready to take on Texas' best on the firing line.

There were forty men on the line at the start of the match, but there weren't more than half a dozen of them that had any chance against me. I reckon offhand that sounds a little like braggin', but it ain't. Most of the men on the line had big bore buffalo rifles. They were fifty caliber and bigger, made for knock-down power, not for accuracy. A few men could hit a target with one of those cannons, but nobody could stand round after round takin' that kind of punishment and keep shootin' against the fine-tuned accuracy of a hand-tooled Tennessee squirrel rifle.

The Preacher's rifle was such a weapon. It was a pointin' rifle. You know what I mean. You took it in hand and it just seemed to come alive. It knew when you were looking at a target. It came to shoulder, then to point, just like a good bird dog. It didn't make any difference whether the man who held it was a snap shooter who liked to fire as soon as he found the target in the sights, or if he was a holder and liked to spend a day and a half squeezin' on the trigger waitin' for the explosion. The gun was pointy and it was steady. I mean the balance was so good, you could take your own sweet time, or point and shoot.

I took count before the match started and found five other Tennessee rifles on the line. A Tennessee rifle didn't have to be made in that state. We called any long-barreled, small-bore percussion rifle a Tennessee rifle just because it seemed the natural thing to call them. Anyway, out of the five, I disallowed two right off. They were beat up and rusty. No man that held his gun in such lack of respect could hope to match

8

Preacher's rifle. I figured there were three of us on the line that might be shootin' all day.

The rules of the match were about as simple as could be. We were divided into groups of three and were shootin' at targets painted on boards. After each round the man that missed the mark the fartherest dropped out of the match. I could see the other fellows with Tennessee rifles were doing the same thing I was. We all made it a point to see that we got matched up with two men with big bores every round. We knew the score from the start, and didn't want to have to face each other too early and maybe let one of those buffalo guns win by default.

There was a few dollars changed hands before the shootin' ever started, but the betting didn't really get to goin' 'til after the first round. After every round the whisky and money were flowin' as fast as the smoke and noise. I kept my own money in my pocket, but a man couldn't help knowin' there was money ridin' on every shot he made. I was used to countin' heavy on my own ability in times of need, but it was a different kind of feelin' to know there were people riskin' hard-earned money on my ability to shoot a hole in a board better than anyone else.

When it came down to six of us still shootin', there were four Tennessee rifles and two buffalo guns. I was surprised, figurin' even those boys without sense enough to take care of their weapons would manage to hold in longer than anybody usin' the big fifty and sixty calibers.

I found myself matched against two Tennessee rifles while a man I had seen around some, Joe Baxter, was matched against the two big fifty calibers. I knew Baxter had a free ticket to the last round, but I would have to work if I wanted to make it. I could see Baxter was all primed to sail on in to an easy victory. I don't know if he had a lot of money bet on hisself or what, but you didn't have to be real smart to tell he wanted to win awful bad. The whole thing didn't mean that much to me. I doubt I would have even entered if it hadn't been for wantin' to show off for that girl. Anyway, I couldn't back out by then. There was money on every man shootin', but you could tell from the noise the crowd was makin', most of it was on Baxter and me.

Somehow, I was still shootin' when it came down to two of us. To be sure everybody was satisfied, the judges brought out new boards for the final round. We took out time to clean our rifles and weigh our powder and shot. There wasn't room for any mistakes that didn't have to be made. I had seen Baxter tippin' the bottle from time to time to steady his nerves. I figured I had him, allowin' gunpowder and whisky make a poor mixture. I couldn't say he was gettin' drunk, but I knew whisky confidence was a false friend when it really counted. I never figured on bein' drunk myself, but I surely was.

I had almost forgotten about the girl. All of a sudden she was right there talkin' to me and me feelin' silly as a school boy.

"I just know we're going to win," she was sayin'.

"You mean you bet money on me?"

"Sure. You can beat him, can't you?"

"I figure I can take him."

"Do you know Joe Baxter?"

"I've seen him around enough to tie his face to his name."

"He don't beat easy. He won the match last fourth of July. And the year before."

"Every man has to lose sometime."

"I suppose."

I found myself resentin' the challenge in her tone.

10

"Sounds like you wish you had put your money on Baxter."

"I guess he's as good as he thinks he is with a gun. There's other things though. He thinks he owns me. There ain't nothing I would rather have him see than me collectin' my winnings after bettin' against him."

There I was. Caught in the middle of a spat between a man and his girl. I would have swore there was somethin' in the way she looked at me. but I guess she was just sizin' me up for the job of makin' her boy friend crawl.

I most surely didn't want any part of that kind of deal, and would have pulled my freight out of there right then if it hadn't been for all the money bet on the outcome of the next round of shots. I had to stick around. Not that I would have run out on my obligation, but if I had tried, those boys with money bet on me would have found a rail and some tar and feathers for my goin'-away present.

Before I knew it, I found myself back up to the firin' line with Baxter standin' on my left. I set my sights on the spot and squeezed as gently on the trigger as I could. Just about everything in the world was goin' through my head except winnin' that match. There was the way the girl had suckered me in; and the wantin' to be gone. and wantin' to win to show her I was the best, and the rememberin' the sweet smell of her perfume. And the sparkle in her eye, not to mention the way her nose kind of pugged on the end and whatever it was inside me that jumped and fluttered around when she smiled at me. And I was so danged mixed up I thought it was all an April fool trick on me instead of the celebration of the Fourth.

And I didn't even know her name.

I reckon the whisky Baxter was drinkin' took up the slack, 'cause he was as far off the mark as I was. Both

11

of our shots drew boos from the crowd. There was enough whisky passin' around and enough money changin' hands to set them on edge. If any of them got it in his head that either of us wasn't tryin' to win, the match would turn into a riot. Baxter and me both settled in for one last shot. He drew aim and fired. He scored the closest to the mark that had been scored the whole day.

I was basically a point-and-shoot type guy. I mean, I didn't find it necessary to spend half a day aimin' at what ever it was I wanted to shoot in order to hit the mark. But I was under the gun, so to speak. If I didn't take all the time my backers thought I needed to beat Joe Baxter, and if I missed, I would suddenly become less than welcome at the celebration.

A man ought to stick to his own way. If I had raised the gun and fired, it would have ended before I had time to lose my aim. The front sight wouldn't settle on the spot. It circled round and round and never would pull in. It was gettin' hotter and I was sweatin' more and the circles weren't gettin' any tighter. I wanted to take the rifle from my shoulder and wipe the sweat off and start all over. But the rules said once a man shouldered his rifle he had to fire or lose his turn. That was to keep the match from takin' all week. Of course it wouldn't have made any difference by the time there were only two of us, but we figured to finish by the same rules we started by.

Sweat ran down into my eyes and I couldn't see a thing. The spot on the board swam in the stingin' brine 'til tears came and washed my eyes out. I blinked a couple times and it felt so good that I closed my eyes for a while. When I opened them, the spot was tryin' to hide behind my front sight. I squeezed the trigger and took the center out of the black mark.

It hadn't occurred to me that the girl might be still

standin' behind me. But before I really realized how good the shot had been, she had me around the neck and was jumpin' up and down hollerin', "We won! We won!" You would have thought she had been sweatin' with me. Maybe she had.

Baxter came over to shake my hand and make the usual gestures to make himself look like a good sport. I didn't know how he would take his girl hangin' onto my neck. It didn't seem to be botherin' him a whole lot as he came toward me. Reachin' out his hand, he said, "I see you've met my sister. Be careful. She won't be as easy to beat as me." He said a lot of other things too, but I wasn't payin' much attention to him.

What ever it was inside me that had been jumpin' around before was goin' wild. Truth was, I hadn't really met Baxter's sister, but I aimed too. That is, if I got the chance. By then there were a dozen men poundin' me on the back and dumpin' mugs of bear on my head and carryin' on like I had done something great, and me knowin' all the while that I was missin' my chance to take the inside track with the prettiest girl I had ever seen . . . at least since I left Missouri.

By and by the well-wishers lost interest in me and went about roundin' up the money they had won on my lucky shot. As soon as they backed off enough for me to sneak between them, I set out to find the Baxter girl. I hadn't made more than a half time around the picnic area when I heard someone callin' my name.

"Laliker. Laliker!"

There wasn't any mistakin' that voice, and it sure wasn't the Baxter girl. Preacher John Mann was comin' bullin' his way through the crowd, splittin' the people like a boulder stands above the water splittin' a mountain stream. And stand above the people, he did. Preacher was six feet ten and three hundred pounds of the ugliest man you ever saw. In that land of big men, he would have been the biggest, had it not been for the one that came in his wake. I never knew the black man by any name other than the given name, Estavan. Whether the name was real or not, the man was. He matched Preacher inch for inch and pound for pound, but he had the classic features of an African king. He was in every way as fine and distinguished lookin' as Preacher was ugly. And the two were inseparable.

They got together nearly a year before out on the staked plains that formed the unmarked and uncertain border between Texas and what was at that time Mexican territory. Out on those plains, they took each other's measure and had formed the kind of friendship that spans any differences of race or position or time or prejudice. After our expedition returned from its venture into Mexico, Estavan rode the circuit with Preacher. And because Preacher loved him, the people of the little congregations accepted him into their homes and meetings. At first he sat quietly in the back of the meetin's and made himself as unnoticed as the laws of nature would allow. By and by he came to join in the congregational singin' and soon became the chior, the song leader, and the soloist wherever the call took the Preacher.

The conquerin' of New Mexico by General Kearny was the salvation of our tradin' venture of the year before, but it also re-opened the Santa Fe trail from Missouri, and brought an end to my plans to open trade routes from Dallas to Santa Fe. Still in partnership with Luke McClure, I took a few wagons south to the coast, hopin' to open up a direct route from the coast to Peter's Colony, but found the shippin' to be too unreliable to count on the coast ports as a source of supply. Seein' a good thing comin' though, I left the Pistalero, Manuel Sainz, to build warehouses and

14

a mercantile on the Galveston bay. But that's a whole 'nother story and I'll tell it some other time.

Anyway, I had just got back from the coast and came to Peter's Colony lookin' for Preacher. I carried his squirrel rifle south with me, kind of like a good luck token, and was usin' the return of it as an excuse for lookin' him up. It's a foolish thing when friends need an excuse to get together. I had just finished a hard drive of more than two hundred miles to return the Preacher's rifle to him, but right then I was more interested in findin' that girl, I didn't even know her first name, than in seein' my old friends.

I did my best to keep from showin' my irritation at havin' my search interrupted, but I never kept anything from Preacher. We grabbed each other like we were old friends and not ashamed to show it in public. He lifted me plumb off the ground and was close to squee-zin' the life out of me before I got my feet back under me. I was countin' broken ribs and grittin' my teeth to keep from showin' the pain I was feelin' as I reached to shake hands with Estavan. I sure couldn't stand a hug like that from him, too.

" . . . did you get in, boy?"

The Preacher's words broke through my concentra-tion. All the while that I had been squeezed close to death, and shakin' hands with Estavan, my eyes hadn't abandoned their search for the girl. I never did like for Preacher to call me "boy," but I never did get up the nerve to challenge him on it, either. I figured he was askin' me the usual questions about the trip, so I covered the best I could.

"We got in last night. Camped on the river a couple of miles south of town, to wash some of the mule off us before we came on in. We had a good trip. Didn't make any money, but we didn't have any trouble we couldn't handle."

15

All the while, I guess I was still searchin' faces in the crowd. We made a little more small talk, then Estavan said, "She was over at the general store a while ago."

Like a fool, I said, "Who?"

Preacher said to Estavan, "I think the boy's turnin' into a barn owl. See the way he keeps rollin' his head around on his shoulders, pokin' his beek this way and that? Now he's even gone to hootin'."

Estavan wasn't havin' any part of Preacher's teasin' me. "Little Annie Baxter, of course. 'Less you already been shinin' up to some other girl since you got back."

So she had a first name. For one of the few times in my life, I couldn't think of a thing to say and was just standin' there feelin' like a fool. Estavan came to my rescue again. "The way them girls flits around like butterflies, you better hurry on over there while she might be still there."

I felt guilty leavin' old friends like that, but both of them understood more of what I was goin' through than I did. "Get on with it," Preacher said. "Are you still camped out on the river? We'll come out to your camp tonight, or the first thing in the morning, for sure. There's more than a few boys got an eye out for Annie. You best get on with first things."

What was there for me to say? I guess they had watched the shootin' match and seen the exchange between the girl and myself. Before I made up my mind to take their advice, they left me standin' by myself in the middle of the crowd.

I didn't find Annie—I was already callin' her by name in my mind—at the store. Nor could I find her back at the picnic. She was so gone from sight that I decided she must have taken off with one of her suitors to share a picnic basket in private.

16

2

The Comanche

There was mourning in the camp of the Comanches. Many good braves lay dead at the hand of the white man. The Laliker. His guns spit death and he had no fear. He held only contempt for the Comanche nation, for he rode alone among them, killing at will, while the arrows and bullets of the Comanche could not touch him. Never had the medicine of the enemy been so strong nor that of the Comanche so weak.

The young braves died and even Standing Bear had narrowly escaped with his life. The Comanche people nursed their wounded and went away from the evil place where the medicine of the white man was so strong. They went northward after the buffalo herds. To follow the way of their people since the first Comanche tasted the flesh of the great hump-backed beast.

But the evil medicine of the one Standing Bear called Laliker went with them. Rivers flooded where always before there had ben only dry stream beds. Even the buffalo were scattered through the land by the evil spell of Laliker. The great herds split into many small bands and moved farther to the north than ever before. The rains kept the strips of flesh from drying into tough jerky. The meat that would have been their winter's food turned green with rot. The women wept and gnashed their teeth, for they knew their babies would starve.

The Kiowa and the Sioux saw the Comanche and that the medicine of the Comanche was weak. They rode through the camps of the Comanche taking food and horses and women, and the medicine of Laliker wet the powder and broke the arrow and the Comanche men died.

Winter's cold breath blew upon the land and there was no meat. No hides for lodges and robes. Not nearly enough horses. There was hunger and disease and cold and hate in the camps. The people called out to their gods for deliverance from the one called Laliker.

Standing Bear walked with a limp through the camps. Once his feet had been the swiftest on the plains. Now any woman could beat him in a race. The bullets of Laliker and his men had torn the flesh and broke the bones of Standing Bear, but they could not kill him. His medicine stood against Laliker's and he lived. He would go and seek out his enemy and they would fight and one would die. But first his people must be taken care of.

Evil medicine walked among them and the Comanche nation was sickened. The heart of the tribe was broken. The proudest of the people of the plains were without the will to survive. But Standing Bear whipped them and shamed them and drove them and they went southward away from the cold breath of winter, far from the land of the Sioux and into and past the lands of the Kiowa. Through the land of the Gringo and deep into the place called Mexico, he drove the people.

The sun was bright and warm and it drove the cold chill from the bones of the Comanche people. They opened their eyes and found the skinny long-horned

18

cattle of the white men and they ate. From the stinking skins of the wooly sheep, they made robes for their backs and blankets for their babies.

The ones who herded the sheep and the cattle screamed their agony to appease the gods of the Comanche. From their blood the Indians took strength and their medicine grew in power. Village after village fell beneath the pounding hoofs of their horses. For every Comanche woman taken by the Sioux and the Kiowa, they took two or more of the dark-haired, bright-eyed Mexican women. Captured Mexican boys filled the ranks of the Comanche braves so thinned since the day of Laliker.

For many moons, they raided and killed and filled their bellies in Mexico. They almost forgot the great herds of buffalo and the way of their fathers. It was good to take from the white man the things they needed. The flesh of the cattle was stringy and had little taste, and the hides were not thick enough to make good lodges. Nor was the hair thick enough nor long enough to make a robe to turn away the cold of winter. But in Mexico there was no winter and the cattle did not follow the call of the Spirit of the North.

There was every day a cow to kill, or a village to raid, or an enemy to defeat. Hunger was a thing they had known in the north, a pain in the insides that grew until it was bigger than the man and consumed every reason for his being and left him dead. It was a thing the Comanche chose to forget. For there was no hunger in this new land. The cattle, the sheep, the women, the children, the corn, the wheat; all the things of the Mexicans were things to satisfy the hunger of the Comanche.

All but one. The hunger of Standing Bear was not for food nor for women nor for horses. It was a hunger for the life of Laliker. Nothing could drive it from him. Though the medicine of the Comanche was again strong, it was not enough. The night time brought to Standing Bear the visions of one riding among his people with rifle and pistol spitting fire and Comanche falling with every shot. Visions of the great black man who had found him, hidden where even an Apache could not have seen him. Visions of those great black hands, with palms paler than any white man's, squeezing from him his very life. Hands that broke his bones like twigs. And the fear he had known and the same in that fear. A hunger of hate and despair and frustration and fear.

The hunger consumed him and made of his eyes bright coals, shining from hollow black sockets. The very flesh of his face and body was consumed. Though he was less than middle-aged, the flesh fell away from his body and his skin was so loose it wrinkled to make him look like an old man.

Many hours each day he sat looking to the north, toward where the great river separated the land of Mexico from the land of the Gringo. The land of Laliker. The wounded of his tribe were healed and seldom did the women weep for the memory of their lost husbands and children. The children ran and played and laughed and forgot the time when cold and hunger left them crying until there were no more tears and on and on until so many passed from among them.

The land that was so good to the Comanche was not good to Standing Bear. Never could his hunger be satisfied south of the great river. But the land of the white man was vast and spread all the way to the East. To where the sun rose each morning from the depths of the great water. Standing Bear would go and search for the hated one. But where? Not in a hundred lifetimes could he search all the land of the white men. Nor could he look into each face seeking that of his enemy. For the Comanche numbered their people by the hundreds and the whites numbered thousands, and thousands of thousands. And when they came, they came in ever more thousands and ripped open the very earth itself to plant their seeds. And all that stood before them fell.

Somewhere among the thousands was the one. And somewhere, sometime, somehow, Standing Bear knew he would taste the blood of his enemy. Even the gods could not keep them apart.

Then came the word. The soldiers of the Mexican army were coming. They came on foot, as many as the trees of the forest. They came on horseback, so many as to spread as far as the eye could see.

Standing Bear went and saw. He moaned in his soul for the good time was gone. Bellies that had been full would be empty. He moaned for the women who would carry the Comanche nation northward on their backs, and for the Comanche men who would die to keep the soldiers from the seed of their nation. And he moaned for the seed. The children who must now go back to the land of the Gringo. To the land of evil medicine. To the land of Laliker.

The woman of Standing Bear lay down her burden beside the trail. For days that had lost number or meaning, the Mexicans pushed them northward, ever northward. Skillful leadership by Standing Bear kept the armies behind the Comanche. When the horse soldiers swung left to go around and cut short their march, Standing Bear set ambush in a canyon and the blood of half a hundred soldiers poured upon the sands and five Comanche women wept and tore their clothes for their men who would never return. Ever northward the Comanche marched and Spotted Fawn lay down and gave forth the son from her womb and the life from her body.

21

The blood of Spotted Fawn stained his hands as Standing Bear held the infant high in the air. He cursed the gods who had taken the life of his woman in exchange for the nothing he held. What good was a son with a twisted foot, one who would never be swift enough to be chief, even among the children. One who would always have a body frail and weak, even as that of his father had become. No, it was not the child of Standing Bear. It was the offspring of the spirit that had plagued them since the first time Laliker rode among them, the evil spirit that had killed them and starved them and had even forced the woman of Standing Bear.

Handing the unwashed infant to the closest women, he said, "Take him away. Never let my eyes see him nor my ears hear his cries. I will never again touch him and never will I hear his name spoken. I will not be told whether he lives or if he dies. But even as it is spirit of the evil spirit, so is it flesh of the flesh of Spotted Fawn. If anyone brings harm to this child, I will know and that person will die by my hand."

There was no respite in the pursuit by the Mexicans. Each day they overtook the Comanche, and each time they were turned back by the cunning of the chief. Ambush and raids on the flank and poisoned water holes kept the armies off balance. But it was the unwillingness of the people to quit that kept them from being pinned down. Like the seed of a watermelon, they squirted out in a new direction each time the Mexicans squeezed them. They went always north.

Twenty days of forced march through Hell, with the bodies of as many braves scattered through the days brought them to the Rio Grande, the great river, a mile wide and a foot deep. Only somewhere in the land of Laliker, storms flooded the mountains and deserts and waters rushed into the streams. The streams over-

22

flowed their banks and vomited their silt and roaring waters into the Rio Grande. And the great river was a rolling, angry barricade. And the Comanche people could go no farther.

As the great bull buffalo of the plains puts his cows and calves within a circle and stands facing off the danger of wolf or lion or storm, so the Comanche men circled round about their women and children. When the armies came they would all die. But they would sell their lives dearly. Many soldiers would go with them to the other side of that river that was greater than the Rio Grande Del Norte.

The soldiers came. They came on horseback and they came on foot. They came from all sides, save the side where the river flowed. They came in squads of ten and in companies of a hundred. They came in a great army of so many that the Comanche had no numbers for them. They came to the beat of unceasing drums and in unending waves. They came with bayonets fixed to rifles. They came with rifles loaded and primed. They came to walk over the Comanche braves, to drive the Comanche forever from their land. To kill the Comanche nation; to cut off their seed.

More than five hundred Comanche followed Standing Bear into Mexico. A hundred and fifty braves stood beside the great chief at the battle of the Rio Grande. The wail of the women was great through the day and through the night. One by one the pounding, hammering, stinking, smoking fire from the Mexican rifles cut the braves down. The raging waters swept away the screaming women and children who ran in panic into the river. And it was over.

The roar of the river died before the light of the sun came. The circle of braves tightened around the women and children. As one body, they moved into the water and across it to the north side. Never had there been a thing like this. Fewer than fifty braves were left, less than a hundred women and children. Even the cold and starvation of the great winter had not been so cruel to them. They were no longer a nation, no longer a people to be feared. They were refugees in their own land. They owned no possessions, save a few horses and what packs the women had managed to seize as they slipped into the water. Impoverished and heart-broken, each man took what was left of his family and went his own way.

The old woman stood beside Standing Bear.

"What will I do with the child?"

"Take it and go."

"My breasts are dry. It will starve."

"Woman, can't you see I don't care?"

"It is your son."

"No. It is the son of the evil spirit. The spirit of the white devil, Laliker."

"You deny your own flesh? Your own blood? Look at him. See the eyes of Standing Bear. See the nose and the mouth. See the great chief he could have been."

"I see the twisted foot and crooked body of a devil."

"Then you see nothing. It is better for the child to die than to grow up hated by his own father. I will throw it into the river."

"No. I forbid its death."

"What would you do to me? I am old and have tasted death many times. My husband and all my children are gone. In four seasons, they have all been taken from me. Do you think I fear anything you could do to me?"

"I am your chief."

"No. You were never chief of the Comanche. You walked tall among us and you said you were a chief and we followed you. Because we followed you, our young men died. The buffalo mocked your hunts. We went hungry and cold and we starved and we froze. We followed you into a bad land and our nation died. No. You are not a chief. *You* are the evil one. It is *you* the spirits hate. You curse the gods of our fathers and we die. You are no longer called Standing Bear. From this day forth you will be called Creeping Snake.''

The old woman spat in his face, then shoved the infant into his arms and turned away.

The spittle dripped from his chin onto the naked baby. There was a sadness deep within him. The pain burned its way upward from the depths of his bowels to his chest. Almost the pain squeezed a tear from his eye. Not since he first earned the right to be called a man had Standing Bear been so nearly a child—or so completely a man. He had decended into the botomless pit. Now he knew. He knew he would climb again into the sunlight. Again, he would be Standing Bear.

3

The Girl is Gone

The word spread through the crowd like wildfire. A hush went before it as people ceased almost even to breathe. Then the truth of the words made its way past unbelieving ears and into everyone's minds. Women cried out and men cursed in their frustrated realization of the tragedy that had come and the pitiful little they could do about it.

Annie Baxter was gone. Her brother, Joe, stumbled into the crowd and, with gasping breaths, told of the Indian who had suddenly raised up before their horses on the trail home. The Indian spooked the horses so badly that Jim was thrown. His head hit a rock and when he woke up, Annie and the horses and the Indian were all gone. He ran all the way back to town for help. No, he didn't know whether the Indian was alone or not. He had only seen the one. No, the tracks didn't go on toward their ranch. They headed West, toward the Llanc Estacado, home of the Comanche and the Kiowa.

I searched the ground around the spot of the ambush. There were things to see—the deep cut tracks where both horses set their hoofs in panicky stop. The rock that took Joe Baxter's senses from him and still claimed his blood, and had probably saved his life.

26

The imprint in the sand where the attacker lay hidden by brush and sand, until the horses were almost upon him. And the tracks of moccasins left so plainly as to dare me to follow after The Other One.

I was shocked by the sudden realization. The attack was a direct strike at me, a move to separate me from the people of the settlement and from the men who drove my wagons. I knew the attacker. A year and more had gone by since I led a train of freight wagons out onto the Llano Estacado, headed toward Santa Fe. On that trip we were attacked by Comanche Indians. The way things happen in battle are seldom planned and I certainly didn't plan to find myself in a position to have to fight off a dozen or more Comanches. That I managed to come out with most of them dead and the others hurtin' and the Indian attack completely routed was purely my good fortune and none of their own. Because they hadn't managed to score even a scratch on me while they were losin' so many braves, I became a sort of token of bad medicine to the whole tribe. They set out to get rid of me in any handy way, and the handiest way was to set the Other One on me. That's the only name I had for him, and I ain't even sure where I picked it up. Anyway there wasn't much he didn't know about hidin' himself in the most unlikely places and bein' where a man would last look for him. And there wasn't much he wanted out of life except my scalp.

I figured I had seen the last of him out on the Llano when he rode away from our wagons, shot more than half to death. Seein' his tracks there and knowin' he had been watchin' while I shot targets and while I made a fool of myself over Annie went straight to my gut. I knew there were two ways I could get the Indian off my back. The first was to kill him. That would be easy enough if I could just get him to show himself at a time when I was armed and ready and expectin' him. But if you figured in the findin' him, sightin' him and beatin' him, then he figured to take considerable killin'. Anyway, it would take a fool to set out deliberately to hunt him down in his own back yard. I didn't like the idea of it at all. But I liked it better than the alternative. The only other way I knew to settle the score was to let him kill me.

Anyway, it looked like he had the deck stacked all the way. He had Annie and he knew, as sure as the sun would rise in its time, I would be on his trail.

The urge to charge out after the Indian burned like a nest of coals deep inside me. But along the way I had picked up a little sense. The Other One held all the high cards. He would pick the time and the place. He would choose the weapons and make the rules. If I took his challenge I would probably die. Holdin' back never entered my mind. But I would do it my way. Not his.

I knew all too well what a delay would cost Annie, and what the possession of a white woman did to an Indian. Not that they thought white women were so special, but they knew what it did to white men. How even the thought of it tore a man's gut out and left him a little less watchful, a little less able to keep his mind on stayin' alive, a little less careful in his movements. Less able to see a back trail, or an ambush. A little more dead.

No. I didn't charge out like the cavalry after the Other One. Other women had been through what she would have to go through. For some it meant the end of life itself. For the stronger women, it meant a horrible time to be endured, then put from the mind forever. I counted on Annie being one of the stronger ones. At best, her only hope of living was for me to stay alive.

28

The Other One would, sooner or later, allow me to catch up to them. A posse of settlers would never manage to stay on his trail. They would fumble around on the prairie until all sign of the passing of the Indian was trampled under the feet of their horses, or be sent in the wrong direction by a false trail laid by the skill of the Other One.

Knowin' first hand the skills of the savage, I knew that only I could save the girl. If that sounds like braggin', then so be it. But how could a posse catch a shadow? How can a man catch the wind? Or find a grain of sand in the desert? No, I couldn't catch the Other One, but he would find me.

It's funny. I never thought of him as a savage 'til he took the girl. Out on the Llano, I thought of him as a Comanche. As a redskin. An Indian. The enemy. The one left behind to kill me. The one older and wiser and more skilful than those who died tryin' to kill me. The one who would never give give up. The one different from all the other Indians. The Other One. But never had I thought of him as a savage.

He was niether primitive, nor wild, nor cruel for cruelty's sake. In that time he was the best-educated man I had ever known. There was no more he could need to know about the land and the animals of the plains. About staying alive, or killin' an enemy. He knew swift, instinctive, reflex action. And he knew the infinite patience of watching for days for his chance to make a kill of animal or man. His skill as a horseman was surpassed only by his stealth and speed and endurance of foot. No. He was never a savage. Not until he laid hands on the girl.

I can't honestly say whether I would have felt different about the matter if I had never known Annie Baxter. But from the moment I saw his tracks in the sand, he was a savage, a thing to be despised. Hunted

29

down Destroyed. I had never known hate before. But then, I had never known love before. The word wouldn't leave me. I didn't know for sure if I loved Annie Baxter. But it was a sudden time in a sudden land. A time when to die a sudden violent death was more likely than the living of a long life. A man slow to make up his mind was likely to never make it up. There was no time for long grudges, nor for long courtships.

And there was no time for day dreamin'. I rode hard for my camp beside the river. I wasn't a man to mistreat a horse, so the teamsters who had drawn watch and stayed in camp knew there was trouble when I came over the ridge, squeezin' the last effort out of a horse who had given all he had and was workin' on that extra somethin' that separates the champion from the ordinary, in horse or man.

They were a good crew and my hurry was theirs. They met me at the cook wagon, ready for any orders I might have. I hit the ground yellin'.

"Sam! Make me up a ten day pack. Grub and powder and shot."

The cook, Sam, didn't waste time with a lot of foolish questions. The job needed doin' and in a hurry. He was already packin' bacon and beans before I finished the order. None of the others was green, either. Mike O'Leary, the wrangler, had the saddle stripped off my horse and was cinchin' it on another one by the time Sam reached the bacon.

"I'll need two pack horses," I yelled at O'Leary.

One pack and two horses meant one would be a "water horse." Someone was already headed toward the stream with two one-gallon canteens in each hand. The men hadn't asked any questions, but I knew the questions that were in all their minds.

"That Comanche that gave us so much hell out in

New Mexico is back. He took a girl out of the settlement. I'm goin' after him." It was a thing any fool could see. They were all ready to go with me, wonderin' why I hadn't asked them.

"Sam, will you follow with your wagon and two or three men?" The answer was only a grunt from the busy man. "O'Leary, bring every horse we can spare from the ramuda." I yelled, turning away from the cook, "This could turn into a long chase. Don't forget extra mules for Sam's wagon." For a lesser man, it would have been an insult to lay out work for him like that. If O'Leary noticed at all, he recognized my need to keep the talk away from the near hopelessness of the thing we were about to try to do.

"Let me try for him by myself," I told those who were grabbing saddles to go with me. "It's me he's after and chances are he'll turn and fight if he sees I'm alone on his trail. I'll leave signs you can follow easy enough. Pick up my trail at morning light and stay at least a day behind me. If I don't catch him by the time I run out of supplies, I'll come back to meet you and we'll work out a better plan."

You could see they weren't too happy about the whole idea, but nobody offered any better alternatives, so they nodded their agreement while I led the loaded pack horses out of camp.

The tracks left by the Other One were gone, wiped out, trampled under the hoofs of half a hundred horses. Of course I knew there would be a posse. The men of Peter's Colony were all of one mind when it came to the protection of the women and children of the colony. It's doubtful there was one among them who wouldn't have died as quickly for the wife or daughter of a neighbor as for his own.

It wasn't in my mind to try to catch them or to try to convince them to turn back. There was that slightest

31

of chances that the posse could overtake the Other One before harm came to Annie. At the best, they would put enough pressure on the savage to keep him movin' and his mind on survival. At the worst they might get too close and cause him to kill the girl to give himself the freedom of movement he would need to escape.

I set my marker for Sam and the others to follow and moved out. There was no reason for me to to follow the posse. I knew where the Indian had come from and where he would go. The Llano Estacado. When a raiding animal makes a kill, whether he's bear, lion, or man, instinct drives him to retreat to home ground. In a war of wits and bullets, a knowledge of the country can be as great an advantage as a company of soldiers. The Other One would use every advantage. He would go home to the plains. I only had about half a million square miles to search. Still, searchin' wasn't the problem. How to stay alive when he found me was my only worry. And Annie.

The Other One led the posse westward through the broken wastelands of Texas. The course he set was as straight and true as an arrow from his bow. He let it be known to me he was headed for the cut in the cap rock wall where I met and fought and killed my first Comanches. We would meet at the rim at the cap, and there the contest would be settled.

A day and a half out of the colonies, the Other One became satisfied I would understand the message left in the direction he took out of the settlements. He turned south toward Mexico and the posse followed like a pack of hounds on the trail of a coon. I was ten days from the Llano by fast saddle horse. The Other One would spend some time laying false trail for the posse. Then he would have to backtrack and some-where leave the false trail before he could turn west again. Of course, he would know short cuts and water holes that I couldn't even guess about. Considerin' his better knowledge of the country and allowin' two days for him to lose the posse, it looked to me like a dead heat in our race to the pass. I had set my mind on makin' the Indian come to me, figurin' that to be my only hope of comin' out of the thing alive. But all of a sudden it seemed mighty important right then to beat him to the Llano.

I stripped packs from both my extra mounts and, carying only saddlebags full of jerky and powder, I set out to beat the Other One to the plains. By switchin' mounts and pushin' as hard as the animals could stand, I knew I could cut as much as three days off the time to get ahead of him and to set up my own ambush.

4

The Kidnapping

He looked upon the caravan of wagons and he knew. They were the same. They were the wagons of Laliker. The seamed and wrinkled face was neather broken by smile nor twisted by frown. The habit of a lifetime's training would not yield. The fallen Comanche chief would show no emotion. Nor would he have been able to describe the feelings burning inside him until they threatened to consume his very soul.

He had no words for the joy of a search ended, a search that might have eaten away at his days until there were none left and he lay old and wasted, waiting only for the spirits to take him.

Where would he have learned words to express the thanks he felt, he who had never needed the gods? He who had fallen on his knees and with his own infant son clutched in his arms had begged for the life of Laliker. He who had scoffed when the medicine men prayed. He who suddenly found his own prayers answered. He who had risen from his knees and mounted the nearest horse and ridden as though guided by an unseen hand straight to the wagons of his enemy.

What emotion could a man show for the thrill of knowing the battle was near and he would soon have his chance to strike down the most hated thing he had ever known? But the same expression must show the fear screaming in his soul, telling him to turn and run, to leave this place, for before him was the dreaded one. The Laliker.

What expression would show the mixture of hate for the one who had ridden knowing and yet unafraid into the Comanche ambush? The one who had calmly sat his horse in the midst of the arrows and bullets. The one who killed Comanche as though they were flies bothering his sleep.

No. There was no expression on the face of Standing Bear. Whether it would be the end of Laliker or of himself, he could not say. In truth, it didn't seem to matter. The only thing important was the ending of the curse. For only in the ending could there be a new beginning for his people.

He watched as the group rode out from the wagons. A dozen men led by Laliker. He saw them cross the stream and ride toward the settlement, the place where white men gathered to talk and trade and get drunk and worship their God. There would be many white men there. But they would be the men who were women, the ones who plowed the fields and tended the cattle. They did women's work and showed no shame. Of these, Standing Bear had no fear. He would walk among them as the wind moves unseen through the trees. And if some fool should by chance discover him, it would be good to cut and slash and leave many dead as the wolf does when it moves through the flocks of sheep.

Standing Bear took from the mare he rode the milk meant for her own foal. Had it been chance or the work of the gods that made him reach out and take the mane of a fresh mare on that darkest of nights? It made no difference. The milk sustained life in the infant. The child of Spotted Fawn lived, though Standing Bear hated the sight and touch and smell of it. He couldn't have answered why he could not abandon the infant, so he never asked it of himself. It was a thing that was there. He fed it. He kept it. He hated it.

Standing Bear placed the cradle board with its burden in the shade of a mesquite bush. If he lived he would return for the child. If not, it would make no difference. The child would never know it had lived or that it had been crippled, or that it had died.

When the rifles barked their thunder and belched their stinking breath, he moved. Many eyes of the white men and of their women passed over the form of Standing Bear. All saw him, but none saw him. He was a part of a tree or a mound of earth. If an eye looked his way, his movement was only a shaking leaf or the settling of dust. Yet when all eyes were on the marksmen or on the marks, he moved.

A few quick steps and he would be upon the enemy. In a flash his knife would strike its blow. It would slide between the ribs and twist and turn, searching out the heart of Laliker. As soon as the white woman moved, he would strike. She was so fair. Her skin was so soft that Standing Bear's eyes could feel the softness as though his hands were touching her. Her laugh rippled through the crowd like the song of a sparrow through the thunderous quiet of the forest. Her eyes sparkled in reflection of joy and happiness incomprehensibly foreign to the way of life known to the Indian. She was so small, yet perfectly complete in all that makes woman to be woman.

There. She was moving away. She no longer blocked his rush. Every muscle tensed. His hand gripped the knife. He started forward. How foolish he had been! He had let his eyes rest upon the woman and had lusted for her. For that he had nearly paid with his life. For there, no farther away than one quick step, stood the giant black man, the same one whose eyes had searched him out of his hiding place on the plains, whose hands had, with so little effort, almost squeezed the life from him. He was stronger than the buffalo bull and quicker than the striking snake, and stood head and shoulders above all the crowd, save one. Beside the Negro stood the very soul and essence of evil itself. It filled the form of a white man, but the ugly features of the evil one marked the face. About the neck was the white band that proclaimed him slave and servant of the white man's God.

Back into the thorny brush he faded. The time was not yet. To kill Laliker was the thing. No matter if he died with his enemy. The only thing he could not forgive himself for would be to die without knowing Laliker would never walk again through his people spreading death and sorrow. He would wait 'til he could be certain, until Laliker was separated from the crowds. Then they would stand face to face and each would live or die by the strength of his own body, and the quickness of hand and cunning of mind.

He watched the woman as she went from the crowd and into the great lodge of many, the place where white men brought out boxes and bags of all manner of things. They filled wagons and carried packages away on foot. Some went in wearing old hats or boots and came out wearing new. Surely this was the place of the white man's God, the church he had heard spoken of.

The woman walked through the doorway of the great lodge. She turned and walked toward Standing Bear as though she meant to challenge him. Her step was straight and unwavering. Drops of sweat broke out under the arms of the Indian. They ran down his side and soaked into his clothes. Had her God told her of his presence? Had the Gods given her some evil medicine to use against him?

Would she strike him dead through some power he could neither see nor understand? Or would she call out to the men? Standing Bear was ready to run. His foot inched up, ready to take the first step at full speed.

Suddenly a hand darted out from the crowd to grasp the woman's arm. She turned and shouted angry words at the man who held her. It was the man who had nearly beaten Laliker in the contest with the rifles. His fine-cut features marked him as the child of the same mother and father as the woman of Laliker. The words the two threw back and forth at each other were harsh on the ears of Standing Bear. But he needed no understanding of the language to know the anger in the words.

Anger was a thing to blind the eye of the most watchful. Surely it wasn't a smile that tugged at the corners of Standing Bear's mouth. Was it a grunt of satisfaction that escaped from within him? He could have made no better plan than what was happening before him. The man almost dragged Laliker's woman to a horse and forced her to mount the animal. Side by side they rode from the crowded settlement.

The Indian slipped from the settlement and headed across country. The road the young couple followed would make a great bend to reach a shallow crossing in the river. Standing Bear raced to get ahead of the horses. The woman would be his. And because the woman was his, Laliker was his. He would come. White men did not share their women. Standing Bear could almost understand the feelings of the white men. He had never shared Spotted Fawn with another brave, and in his refusal he knew the anger of those who had shared their squaws with him. But he didn't care. Like a good horse, she was his and no other man had ever used her.

Laliker's woman would be the same. She would be the bait to draw Laliker away from the rest of the white men. Many would come after them, but as the days went by the others would fall away and only one would follow. Then Laliker must face him alone in the land where they had first met.

Almost before he could hide himself, the horses carrying the two came around the bend. They were upon him and he exploded from hiding with a war scream and throwing a great cloud of dust. The horses panicked into a wild circus of bucking and twisting to rid themselves of their riders so they might escape the terrible thing the ground threw in their faces. Joe Baxter lost his seat and his head smashed against a rock. His world went black, as the blood flowed from the open wound. Only the quick hand of the Indian as it grasped the reins of her horse kept Annie from suffering a similar fate.

The screaming girl was quieted by a blow from the hand of her new master. She sat her saddle quietly as the Indian mounted her brother's horse and led her away. Her mind raced in circles without finding comfort. Her brother Joe was dead. Nobody could be hit so hard, or bleed so much, or lie so still and yet live. How long before they came for her? Too long. The celebration would last into the night. All her neighbors were already at the picnic. Only if a chance stranger came along would Joe's body be found before dark. It would be daylight before a search could begin. And that would be too late.

No woman lived in Indian country without wrestling with the question of what they would do if they were ever captured by Indians. Many placed more value on their bodies than on their lives—at least they thought they did. They swore to kill themselves rather than submit to the Indians if captured. Some even carried in their clothes a hidden gun or knife to use on themselves. More often than not, they attempted to use the weapon on their captors instead of themselves. Annie was one of the few who admitted a love for life that would let her endure whatever might come. She had no visions of taking her own life to protect her body. She scorned the carrying of weapons for such a purpose. But how she wished for some weapon, a knife or a gun, anything to strike out at the one who held her and had murdered her brother.

The cries of the infant penetrated her thoughts. They seemed to be coming from a thicket of mesquite ahead of them. The Indian rode to the thicket and dismounted. Annie screamed to warn what she thought must surely be a young mother tending her child on the far side of the brush. Her screams brought only the threat of another blow from the raised fist of the Indian. The cries continued and Annie watched in amazement as the ugly Indian brought forth the child.

He handed the baby to the girl and made noises she could not understand. There was no mistaking his demands, though, when he ripped at the front of her dress and pushed the child's head against her breast.

"I can't," she cried. "I don't have milk for your baby."

Standing Bear raised his hand to club her into submission. The rage in his face told the girl he was without control of his mind. She opened her dress and placed the tiny mouth over her breast. The crying stopped and deep within the young woman some deep emotion stirred.

Night took them to a campsite near a trickling spring. There was no food, but the water was sweet on the girl's lips. Her swollen tongue soaked up the water as she swallowed great gulps. After the horses were watered, she washed her own face, then unstrapped the baby from the board it was bound to, gagging at the stench that came from the child's wrappings. She threw the board and wrappings as far from the camp as her strength would allow. She missed the grunt of satisfaction that escaped Standing Bear. He knew the discarded cradle board would cause confusion for his enemies. And the more problems the white men had to worry about, the better his chances of fooling them became.

Annie bathed the tiny body. The sight of the club foot brought tears to her eyes. Her petticoats were torn into diapers and blankets for the baby. There was no food for the starving infant. Desperately, the girl hoped that somehow the child might make it through the night. To quiet the hunger cries, she again opened her dress and placed the mouth over her nipple. Again the emotions stirred deep within her body. They slept.

The sun found them many miles from the spring. Already the day's heat was drawing the moisture from Annie's body. The pain of hunger burned in her stomach. She cried for the child dying in her arms. Tears freely flowed from her eyes as she silently wept for the baby. Why it had not died during the night, she could not understand, but she knew starvation would overcome and the child would die.

There was little sign of life left in the child when they found the flock of sheep. There were hundreds of the woolly animals with no shepherd. The minutes seemed like hours while the girl sat gently rocking back and forth, comforting the infant that could no longer cry. From the rim of the ravine which concealed them and their horses, Standing Bear watched the flock.

No dog barked nor man moved. At long last, the decision was made; the sheep were not tended. Still he watched. And then he was gone. Annie didn't see him slip over the edge of the ravine, but gradually she was filled with the feeling of being alone. She looked to where he had been concealed a few minutes before and found the place empty. She was alone. But not quite alone. Occasionally a spasm jerked the tiny body she held clutched in her arms. The face wrinkled and the mouth opened, but no sound came out. She was free. Fear of her savage captor drove at Annie. *Run. Go. Escape.* But she could not. The flicker of life still in the child held the woman inside her bound tighter than any rope or chains could have. She couldn't leave the baby, and to take it with her would be to kill it. Impossible as it seemed, there was hope for the baby. But the hope was not a thing she could take with her. She couldn't find food for the baby. The man could. If the Indian came back, and if she could make him understand, he could find milk for the child. She was torn between a lifetime of hate and prejudice and stories of the foul, evil ways the Indians treated women, and the longing for the life of the child. In hysterical panic, she feared both that the Indian would return, and that he would not.

5

The Posse

Joe Baxter would not hear their arguments. He was going with the posse, and that was final. It was his sister the Indians had taken. By the blood that flowed through his veins, and Annie's, he swore to find her. And from the hate that filled his heart and soul, he swore vengeance on anyone who dared lay hand on a Baxter woman.

The horses that gathered around the blood-covered rock, fresh and high-spirited and anxious to run, tramped out any evidence of how many Indians there had been. The only tracks leading away from the scene were of Baxter's own horses.

The posse threatened to turn into a circus as a dozen young men who had each harbored visions of winning the affections of Annie Baxter shouted for a headlong charge after the heathens. Wiser heads called for bringing an Apache tracker. How did they know it wasn't Apaches that had taken Annie? Somebody hollered for the army.

Another voice ridiculed the one calling for the army. "Do you want to wait for the soldier boys to come all the way from Fort Gibson?"

"Hell, no. Ain't you heard? There's a Major Arnold got some soldiers thirty or forty miles southwest of here. Calls it Camp Worth. Bet he's got Indian scouts, too.''

"Yeah. And maybe his scouts is the ones that's got Annie."

"No soldiers." The voice was Joe Baxter's. "The army wants to make pets out of the Indians. The Indians that took Annie ain't gonna be nobody's pets."

Nobody questioned the meaning of his words or the look on his face. Nor did they question his right to veto calling out the army.

The lull after Baxter's proclamation gave the Preacher the chance he had waited for. He took charge of the mob.

"Everybody that has extra saddle stock or guns, go get them. If you don't have enough powder and shot to last you through a siege, go get what you need at the store. Those that ain't goin' after horses or weapon's, go with Tailor. Y'all pick up supplies at the store and head back here. Get enough food and supplies for twenty men for more than a week."

"Who's gonna pay for all that?" It was Tailor's question and Tailor's right to ask it. He ran the store and would be accountable for the merchandise. "That will be a wagon load. It will cost more than my wages for a month."

"Put it on the Baxter account." Young Joe Baxter claimed the liability.

"No," Preacher said, "put it on everybody's bill. Equal shares for every family in the colony. It'd be a bad thing if next time a thing like this happens it's to someone who can't pay and nobody goes out to help because there ain't no supplies. Estavan and me ain't got any money, so we'll work our shares out among the families."

The people knew the Preacher would more than work out his share, and Estavan the same. No family

44

on Preacher's circuit had missed having the two giants as "guests" on their farms. When those two set to work it was like a whole crew had come onto the place. The Preacher could coax more work out of a team or mules or yoke of oxen than any other man in the colonies. When it came to hauling hay or digging a well or clearing stumps or rocks from a field he was worth two, maybe three, ordinary men. Estavan would not work in the fields, but his hands were those of a master. In them raw wood took on the shape of table and chair or cabinet or hutch. Sick or lame animals responded to his soft words and gentle touch. And the sick were healed and the lame walked. So nearly miraculous was was the touch of Estavan that had the gift been in the hands of another, Preacher might have called it witchery. But he knew there was no room in the heart of his friend for evil.

"O.K., move out." Preacher shouted the command. "Me and Estavan and Baxter will follow the tracks. The rest of you catch up when you can, but don't expect us to wait for you."

Of the trio, the job of tracking fell naturally to the huge black man. If the job had called for reading words from a printed page, either of the others might have been better able to fill the bill. Or maybe they couldn't. On many unguarded moments, more than a hint of education showed through the mask of ignorance the man wore, just enough to make those who knew him best wonder at his past. And he spoke Spanish as well as any of the Mexican residents. Even French words rolled off his tongue sometimes. But the story written in the sand and on the rocks was not for the casual reader. It was written only for the sharpest eye, backed by the education attained in the university of survival.

And well he read it. Slowly at first, he led his mule

while trained eyes searched the ground for signs of trickery. Satisfied at last, he mounted up and trotted the mule along the trail of the girl and her captor.

The story was of a wide swing back toward the settlement, where they stopped to pick up something left hidden in the brush. Then as straight as the terrain would allow, the trail led west and south.

By nightfall the posse had grown to ten men and a remuda of twenty or more spare mounts. To be sure they didn't trample out the trail, they backtracked a quarter mile before making camp. By then it was well established that a lone renegade held Annie. But all the helpless posse could do was to wait for daylight, and agonize in their hearts for what they knew Annie Baxter must be suffering at the hands of the renegade.

There was little more than absolutely essential conversation. Every ear was straining for sounds carried on the winds saying Annie was just a short distance out in the brush where a charge by the posse would overwhelm the Indian and rescue the girl. No such sound came. No more fruitful were the eyes that strained for a glimpse of a flicker of light saying, "Out here is a campfire. Come and strike down the redskinned devil." No wisp of smoke rode the breeze calling the posse. But the lack of reward did not dull the senses of the searchers. It honed them to a razor sharpness few of the men had ever felt before. Like a wolf pack thirsting for the blood of elk or deer, they thirsted for the blood of the Indian.

Daylight found the posse, now twenty men strong, a beehive of turmoil as horses were roped and saddled and topped off. The dust in the air gave grit to the bacon and steaks that sizzled in the great cast iron skillets. Dutch ovens yielded hard-bottom biscuits and the eternal pot of frijole beans simmered at the edge of the fire.

Like a great arrowhead, the posse pierced the vast unsettled lands. Estavan was the tip of the arrow as his tracking skill guided the band of avengers. Over rocky hills and through dry arroyos where most of the men could see no sign of the passage of the Indian and his captive, Estavan led without waver or hesitation.

Behind Estavan rode the Preacher with Henry Tucker at his side. Tucker was a hollow-eyed man whose mind was consumed and overflowing with hate. Many men in Texas at that time muttered that the only good Indian was a dead Indian. When Henry Tucker made such a statement, he was dead serious. And more than a few Indians became good Indians at the hand of Tucker.

Tucker's hate was not without reason. A little over a year before, a raiding party of Indians had taken his daughter, Irene. Though they found the girl some days later, she had left her mind and her beauty and her eyesight on the plains. Henry Tucker hated. Every time word came to him of Indians passing through the area, Henry Tucker hunted. In the months after he lost Irene, twenty-seven Indians paid the price for what they'd done to Tucker's daughter. Six were shot dead while they moved in the light of their camp fires at night. Four were found mutilated, scalped, and throats slashed short distances from their camps. Several had been roped and dragged to death through the thorny mesquite and rocks of the country. But the ones who paid the most were the ones who were captured and tied to cactus and whipped till there was little skin left to cover their bones. Tucker's knife made short work of their manhood and a burning stick left them as blind as Irene. Each time an Indian thus mutilated was found by white men, many wagging tongues whispered, "Tucker" but there was no proof. And fewer and fewer Indians ventured near the white settlements.

Farther back in the posse rode Willie Wilson. Wilson's son died on the night Irene Tucker was captured. Had he given his life defending the girl? Surely he had. At least Wilson believed so over those long months. The mothers of the young people believed so, too. They took comfort in each other's grief. Mrs. Wilson had spent many hours in the months past, relieving the girl's mother in tending her. And many more hours as the two women sat side by side saying little, but each allowing the other to draw strength from her presence.

It wasn't the same for the men. Henry Tucker made no secret of placing the blame for what befell his daughter. If she hadn't been out walking with the Wilson boy, she would be alive. Tucker considered his daughter to be dead. When the blame fell on the son, it fell on the father. The colt is no more or less than the sire. If the boy had never been sired, Irene would be alive.

Willie Wilson had seen several of the mutilated bodies of the Indians over the months, and two of the living dead. Others suspected Tucker, but Wilson knew. The cold, hollow eyes of the man told of an insatiable, insane hatred. And to be kept alive, a hatred must be fed. When the eyes turned upon him, Wilson had no doubt that sooner or later he would be consumed by that hatred. He could only hope Tucker would be killed by one of his intended victims. But he knew the time would come when he would have to kill the man or die. And he was neither a murderer, nor a skilled fighter. Wilson feared.

Manuel Ortiz rode with the posse, yet alone. The Spanish blood that flowed through his veins carried with it the blood of an Indian grandmother. The constant talk of ''Murdering savages, filthy redskins, butchers, and heathens'' tore at his mind. ''You're wrong,'' he wanted to scream at them, but the words would not come. If to be Indian was to be savage, then he, Ortiz, must be a savage, too. But it was a lie. There was nothing savage about the woman who had held him while he was a child, nor the people of her village where he had visited so many times as a youth.

Ortiz knew the meaning of the word savage, for he, too, had looked into the eyes of Tucker. He had seen Tucker's eyes and the hunger in them as they looked upon his dark skin. He had watched as Tucker looked upon the other Spanish-speaking people who had first settled the area. The skin and hair of most was nearly as dark as that of the Indians. Ortiz, like Wilson, knew the truth of the rumors about Tucker. The only thing he didn't know was how long it would take the sick mind of the man to decide that all Mexicans were truly Indians and in need of punishment.

Ortiz knew.

Bob Cooley rode among the younger members of the posse. Twice in a year the young man had seen the object of his fantasies carried off by Indians. From afar, he had worshipped first Irene Tucker, then Annie Baxter. Neither ever knew of his affections; for how does one speak to the most sought after girls in the county through a harelip that left him believing himself to be the butt of every joke? He couldn't have either of the girls, but he had known them in his dreams. He had dreamed of riding in among all the boys who constantly courted the favors of the beautiful young ladies and dreamed of their rejection of the tall handsome young men with their silver-tongued blarney. He had dreamed of being picked from among all the young men to share the life of so rare a woman that she could look beyond the handsome faces and smooth tongues.

Life denied Bob Cooley all the things it had given

most young men. Now the Indians had taken from him even his dreams. Cooley's new dreams sent him riding among the Indians, killing and slashing and shooting. He would rescue Annie, and she would know he was the best man and she would be his. Bob Cooley dreamed.

From the hatreds and fears, the knowledge and the dreams of men come the victories and defeats of mankind. Most of the men who followed the Negro and the Preacher across the plains of Texas were settlers and buffalo hunters, family men who rode out of a sense of duty and because they knew that if ever this same tragedy befell them, their neighbors would not hesitate to ride out after the renegades. Like most people, they had no way of knowing where the hatreds and fears and dreams of the few would take them.

It was midafternoon before they found the abandoned cradle board and the foul wrappings that had held the infant son of Standing Bear. The minds of the men puzzled over the mystery. How had a child so tiny come into the possession of the renegade Indian? Was the child the spoil of a previous raid? Why had it not been killed? How had it survived without a woman to feed it? Was the child the reason the Indian had taken the white woman? What would happen to Annie when the infant died? For die, it surely would.

Estavan pondered all these things in his mind, and his heart softened toward the red man. A little less, he hated the man he swore to kill.

That the tiny spring had offered shelter and water for the Indian and his captive through the night was obvious to all. And that they had gained no closing of the distance between them and the renegade was also obvious. He was still as far ahead as he had been from the time the posse set out on his tracks. But they

were not surprised by this. Their only hope of catching
the Indian was in their greater numbers and the remuda
of fresh mounts. As the days passed, the horses of
Annie and the Indian would falter and then fall.
Though the Indian might manage to escape on foot,
he could never take the girl and child with him.

How many days would it take? Two? Three? Four?
The time would pass and the Indian would either free
his captive, or kill her.

6

Annie and the Indian

Standing Bear drove the four sheep up the narrow draw to where he had left Annie and the infant. Annie's stomach drew into a knot at the thought of food. Hunger had been her companion almost as constantly as fear from the time of the surprise attack. But as hungry as she was, she knew she was not yet near danger of starving. Not so for the child in her arms. Almost joyfully, she grabbed the nanny goat that led the sheep.

Hands that had a thousand or more times drawn milk from cows, had no trouble drawing milk from the goat. If she had cared, Annie would have known the goat was the milk-goat of the lonely shepherd. The animal offered no resistance.

Annie had no bucket to catch the milk so she first tried to squeeze the life-giving liquid directly into the mouth of the baby, but the child only gagged and spit it out. Even in the hopelessness of her situation, Annie's thoughts carried her back to her father's farm and milking time. How she wished the baby was one of the numberless cats that always hung around the barn begging for milk. And how they sputtered and sneezed but still tried to catch the stream of milk Annie would squirt at them when her father wasn't looking. Desperately, the girl searched for a container, but there

52

was nothing. Finally, she held a cloth, the last clean piece of her petticoat, in one hand while she squeezed the milk onto it. When it was soaked, she gave a corner to the Indian baby and it fed. Over and over, she soaked the cloth and over and over the near-starved infant sucked the milk from it.

The sheep stood in silence as Standing Bear moved among them. With deft strokes of his razor-sharp knife, he slit each throat. Almost as quickly, he peeled the skins from the carcasses. In amazed despair, Annie watched as he wrapped the hoofs of the horses in the skins. The wooly side of the skin was left on the outside. As the hoofs gained their new boots one by one, their tracks disappeared. Where before they had cut sharp and distinct tracks in the soft dirt, now they left no more than a smudge in the sand.

A good tracker might still follow the hoof marks, but only if the horses never left soft sand, and only if no breeze blew and the eye never blinked. To lose the trail once would be to lose it for good.

The juices of the nearly raw meat flowed down her throat and again brought spasms to Annie's stomach. Knowing she would only heave the meat up if she ate it too fast, she pulled at it with her fingers. It refused to separate. Looking across the fire at the savage, she recoiled in disgust. Like a mongrel dog, the man held a great chunk of meat and gnawed on it. Blood and tallow ran down his face and soaked the front of his clothes.

Never, she thought! I won't let this land or this man made a savage of me. If I have to starve, I won't eat like an animal. She was too shocked to react when the man handed her the knife from his belt. Calmly, she sliced bite-sized pieces from the still roasting meat. Not till afterward did she wonder what would have happened if she had tried to use the knife as a weapon against her captor. Still later she wondered how many human throats the knife had cut, and how many scalps it had separated from their owners.

The dirt banks of the arroyo were undercut by rushing water in dozens of places. Standing Bear threw the remains of the sheep he had butchered into one of the cuts and made short work of kicking the creek bank down on top of the bones. He loaded the meat trimmed from the bones onto his own horse and forced Annie to mount the other. When she was mounted, he tied the nanny goat across the back of her saddle like a blanket roll. The bleating goat was quieted by a blow between the eyes by his fist.

The Indian scattered the flock of sheep as much as he could, driving most of them over the spot where they had camped.

Leading the way through the midst of the flock, Standing Bear made a great circle toward the south, then back toward the Llano. Not until there was a sheet of solid rock beneath the horses' hoofs did the Indian leave the flock.

The day was gone and the night and much of the next day before the layers of sheepskin wore through and again the horses tracked the land. By then, Standing Bear didn't care. No tracker could follow so many miles without tracks. Only at the caprock would it again make a difference. It would not do for Laliker to find his tracks and turn the trap he would set against him. But the skins wrapped around the meat would be enough to again cover the hoofs of the horses. The trap he would set would be death for Laliker. There must be no mistake.

More than an hour's ride from the caprock that rose above them, Standing Bear halted. To ride under the rim rock, exposed to the light of day and whatever enemies that might be hiding on the rim would be foolish. Standing Bear was not foolish.

He hid his horses and captive in a shallow buffalo wallow and worked his way on foot to high ground. For the first time he felt it necessary to tie the woman before leaving her. With the goat to feed the baby, she might attempt to escape. The thought was close to a hope in the Indian's mind. Almost, he left her unbound, but could not. If she managed to reach Laliker, the trap would never close and the evil medicine of the white man would continue to work its spell on the Comanche people.

Through the day the eyes of the Indian searched the rim of the Llano. He saw no movement that might be a man. Nor was there a flash from the sun glancing off a gun barrel.

In the last hours of sunlight, the Comanche walked a great arc beneath the wall of stone. Nowhere was there track of horse or man. At last, satisfied that he had reached the caprock ahead of Laliker, he returned to his camp.

In the near darkness after the setting of the sun behind the caprock, Standing Bear replaced the wornout sheepskins on the horses' hoofs with fresh ones. Then, in a hurry to beat the rising of the moon, he pushed his captive toward the caprock.

The spring was really more of a seep and it lay far back in a box canyon that twisted several times before it opened onto the rolling plains below the cap. It was so well hidden that the Indian felt no hesitation in starting the fire. The woman would not eat the meat uncooked and even to him it was begining to taste foul from the sun's heat. It would be good to roast the meat again.

Even with a fire to cook the meat Annie demanded the knife from Standing Bear and trimmed away the green parts before she skewered the flesh with a cedar branch and held it over the fire. The Indian grunted his disgust at the wastefulness of the white woman. A good squaw would break her of her foolishness in short order.

Through the days, Annie kept the infant constantly in her arms to protect it and to know its every need. Through the nights, she held it like a shield between herself and her captor. Each time the man seemed ready to force himself upon her, she clutched the child tightly to her breast and faced him down. The milk of the goat brought miraculous new life to the infant. Though the amount of milk the little animal gave each day had decreased much since she was forced to travel so hard on so little water, it was enough. The rich fat in it even added flesh to the tiny bones and sparkle to the eyes. But it couldn't straighten the crooked foot of the infant. Nor could it straighten the hate-twisted face of the man.

The fire burned low and the woman sang soft lullabies to the tiny life that had become a part of her and was both her ward and her protector. When she allowed herself the luxury of remembering home and family, she found it hard to keep her mind off Irene Tucker. Was it just a year ago the Indians captured her? Pretty Irene, with hair so blonde and skin as soft as the velvet petal of the wild rose. Folks first said she ran off with the Wilson boy. Then a week later the stink led them to the boy's mutilated body, less than a hundred yards from the Tucker house. It was the work of Indians. There was no question from the start. Poor Irene. There was no sign of the girl. The posse went out more to ease the mind of the girl's mother than with hopes of finding her. To everyone's surprise they did find her. It was three days later and she was wandering naked on the plains. The skin that hadn't been stripped from her with whips was so badly sunburned it was covered by great running blisters. The once beautiful face was all one big sore with blind eyes staring from it. Since that day, Irene had spoken no words and the eyes had never closed, not even in sleep.

How long had it been? More than a week? Yes, Annie told herself, she had been a captive longer than Irene. But she still had her mind and her body, thanks to the baby. Or did she? Was she as crazy as Irene? Was the baby real or was it something an insane mind had given her to protect her from knowing? What difference did it make? Whether it was real or a thing in her mind, she had the baby. She sang another lullaby.

Standing Bear looked upon the woman. She was pleasing to his eyes. Given enough time and sun, the skin that was so white would darken to a more pleasing color. But would it stay so soft? The memory of her struggling in his arms and the soft feel of her flesh sent a heat rushing through his body. Even Spotted Fawn had not been so soft. Especially her hands. The baby softness of her hands was an amazing and thrilling thing to the Indian. The hands of a squaw were hard and rough and calloused and cracked. Even the hands of a very young girl were harder than a man's. Woman's work was a thing that hardened the skin and cracked it and made it tougher than the leather of a moccasin. But the hands of the woman who held his child were as soft as the skin of the child itself. It was no wonder the touch of her hand brought peace and quiet to the child.

Looking at her across the fire, he made a decision. He would keep her. He had meant only to hold her long enough to use her as bait for Laliker. When Laliker was dead, and he was otherwise finished with her, he had planned to kill her. But no. There was a thing about her. She would be his squaw. She would never be worth so many ponies as Spotted Fawn, but she was so soft.

The metallic clicking sound meant nothing to Annie. It was a sound she had heard so many times that it had become a part of her life. Her other life. Before the Indian. She wouldn't have noticed it at all if it hadn't been for the reaction of her captor.

In a single motion, he threw his robe over the remnants of the fire and sprang to his feet. Hands grabbed her, pulling her up and shoving her into the darkness at the same time. She was astride the horse, with the goat on behind before the meaning of the sound penatrated her consciousness. It was the sound of a revolver cocking, with the cylinder rolling into place. Someone had come for her. It could have been another Indian out there, a Kiowa or even an Apache. No! As surely as the sun had set, the man was white. And he had come for her. She would not let herself believe otherwise. She struggled against the Indian. She must delay. Was it a posse? Or Joe? How had they found her? The Indian's fist cut off the scream she hadn't even realized was coming from her own throat.

With a fury, the Indian drove his captive out onto the Llano. Insanely he cursed himself for allowing Laliker to come upon him. Never for a moment did he doubt the identity of the one in the dark. Who else but Laliker could follow tracks that were not there? Who else had such strong medicine against the Comanche that he could find a camp hidden even from his own people? And who else carried a revolver that fired so fast and never missed though no aim was taken? No one but Laliker.

Fear drove its icy wedge into the heart of the Indian. Fear for the Comanche people. If need be he would gladly die to see Laliker dead, but what if he failed? How could a man fight the evil medicine of Laliker? No Comanche bullet or arrow could strike him. No Comanche cunning or skill could bring him into striking distance. Always just as the knife was raised or the weapon aimed, the evil one who protected Laliker sent someone to upset the trap or even to kill the attacker.

The Comanche people must live. If his thoughts had not been on the woman, even Laliker could not have surprised him. Knowing his weakness calmed the fear within him. He would rid himself of the weakness, but he could not abandon the woman and his own child to die on the plains. They must have water and food and a chance to survive. No man had ever been promised more by the spirits.

7

Laliker Alone

Far to the South, I could see the flicker of a camp fire. It was twenty miles or more away and visible to me only because my camp was on the highest ground I could find. Probably the posse had done the same. While my motive had been to gain a better view, I reasoned that they had chosen their position on high ground, easy to defend, in case the Indian had led them into a trap.

Doubts pulled at my nerves. What had made me so sure it had been the Other One? I searched my mind for a picture of a recognized track or something dropped. There was nothing. Only the impression, a gut feelin'. The knowin' was no longer so positive and the feelin' no longer so strong. I longed to be with the men of the posse. Surely they would run the renegade to the ground. I picked up my tack and carried it to the freshest of my mounts. I dropped the gear into a tangled pile and separated out the bridle.

The bay geldin' rolled his eyes at me like he was thinkin' I had lost my mind. To him the hobbles and picket rope signaled the end of the day's work. But there I was, fightin' him to take the cold steel bit when he'd earned the right to graze and drink and sleep through the night. How could he understand when I suddenly pulled the bridle back off and left him standin' as I carried my saddle and gear back to the remains of my camp fire? I wasn't sure I understood myself. But I couldn't shake off the feelin' that the Indian was the Other One and we were destined to meet on the Llano.

The days that followed became an endless race. Almose hourly I switched mounts. By the third day, my water and food supplies had shrunk to a one-horse pack. Endlessly I consumed the miles until the great wall of the caprock stood before me—the sheer embankment that marked the eastern boundry of the Llano Estacado. Like the earth itself had split and one half had raised itself high above the other, it stood towerin' hundreds of feet before me.

I knew that somewhere to the south the wall wasn't so high, nor so steep. The years and weather had sent the rocks rolling down until there was almost a gentle slope up which wagons had gone. It was where I had first met the Comanche and where the Comanche had died, the place where I had first faced the Other One, and where I would wait for him.

It wasn't hard to find a dead end canyon, narrow enough at the neck to be easily fenced, yet with grass and water enough to last my horses for many days. It was more of a barricade than a fence that I built across the mouth of the canyon. I stretched my lariat across most of the distance and tied it between two cedars. Then, like a woman hangin' clothes on a line, I draped the rope with cedar branches. Where the rope failed to reach the canyon wall, I filled with scrub cedars piled loosely. An hour's work satisfied me that the horses would stay put. The last thing I wanted was to fence the animals in so tight they couldn't escape if a cougar found them, or if I didn't make it back and the grass and water supply ran out.

I worked southward as I made my way up the canyon wall. My idea was to top out well north of the cut in the wall where I expected to meet the Other One. I knew I might be as much as a day's walk from the cut, but the one thing I didn't want was to lay tracks anywhere near there for the Indian to find. By workin' in from the northwest, I was sure he couldn't reach my tracks without crossin' in front of my gun.

I nearly outsmarted myself on that deal, though. The climb and the walk took most of two days and left my canteen nearly empty. There wasn't any doubtin' my ability to make it back to the horses if I headed back right away. But what would I do if it was two or three or a dozen days before the Indian came! If I waited too long to head back, I'd never make it. But I had already gambled too much on my hunch to do anything but wait.

Of course there were my own men, following with supplies and horses. Chances were good they would interpret the signs right and follow with water. If not, and if I stayed on the rim of the cap more than a day, I was a dead man.

Somehow the whole thing struck me funny. I couldn't help laughin' at the thought of the Other One comin' in a week and findin' me there, dead in the pass. I reckon it was a choice between laughin' and cryin'.

The night passed and the followin' day stretched westward. Around noon the last of my water was gone. Thirsty as I was, it was a hard thing to pour that last bit of water into my mouth. A voice inside me kept tellin' me to save some back, but that was ridiculous. A grown man's body is goin' to use close to a gallon of water every day. If it don't get the water from outside the body, it will draw it from his own flesh. No one will ever know the number of men who have died of thirst with a pint or more of water still in their canteens, men that saved their water while their own bodies cannibalized them. Still, it was with regret that I poured the last of the water into my mouth and swallowed it down.

I had plenty of jerked beef and kept a chunk in my mouth most of the time after the thirst got to workin' on me. Chewin' on the tough meat drew moisture into my mouth and lessened the awareness of the thirst that was slowly killin' me.

Hidin' in the shade of scrub cedar or rock, hopin' the glare of the sun was not reflected from the lens of my binoculars, I waited and watched. For two days, I watched every pronghorn, every coyote, every critter the size of a jack rabbit or bigger. Not even the wind moved without drawin' inspection from my searchin' eyes. Still, another night came and the enemy did not.

My thoughts wouldn't stay away from the sweet waters that filled the lake somewhere out on the Llano. Sweet cool water flowed from the springs of the white caliche rock clifs the Mexicans called Los Portales. The porch. The Portales. The gateway to life itself. For through those rock portals flowed the water that was life to countless creatures of the plains.

How far to the springs? Too far. Days, or weeks. More likely an eternity. Who except the scout Ramirez could find the valley of the Portales in the vast expanse of the Llano?

The Other One could. He would pass here and find my body and laugh and take Annie to the Portales.

When the moonless black of the night made my vigil useless, I went out in search of water. An hour from my hidin' place had me crawlin' more than I walked. The canyons and breaks, the rough country, called the caprocks, was more rugged than most mountains. I was on top, on the edge of the Llano Estacado where side canyons and breaks and washes and gullies plowed the ground into a treacherous, continual trap. Any wrong step would send the rocks rollin' from beneath my feet and my body plungin' hundreds of feet to the canyon floor. It was no place to be strollin' around in the black of the moon on feet too weakened from thirst to manage more than a shufflin' stagger. So I crawled.

I moved south along the rim, chewing on the pulp of every soft vegetation my hands touched. Most I spat out in disgust at the bitter taste. But, like an animal, I consumed the few that offered any moisture I could swallow. I couldn't keep stories of poison plants and the mind-stealing peyote and loco weeds out of my thoughts, but I was past the point of caution. Without some kind of moisture, I was dead already. What difference did it make if I poisoned myself?

I came against a wall of rock that, in the dark, might have been a giant boulder or the canyon wall itself. But it couldn't be the canyon wall. I was on top. The wall of the canyon fell away from me on my left. Like an omen, the boulder blocked my way and I could go no farther. To go around it would send me so far from a straight line course I would have to wait for daylight to find my way back to my lookout point. And I meant to be back on the point long before that. I used the rock wall to pull myself to my feet and turned back to the path I had just covered.

I turned an inch or a foot or a yard too far and stepped into the empty void of black nothing.

I was alive. Or was I? I couldn't tell whether the pain and nausea and the spinnin' star-filled sky were real or the outskirts of Purgatory. How long did they say? A thousand years? Or was it ten thousand years the soul would be tortured in Purgatory? There. That sound. The bleatin' of a goat? Or the cloven-hoofed Prince of Darkness? The smell of fire and brimstone. And the soft singin' of an angel comforting a lost soul in the pits of darkness.

The next I knew, the stars were no longer spinnin' in the heavens and the moon flooded the land with light. The pain still wracked every inch of my body, but my head was clearer. I remembered the fall, but wasn't sure whether I had simply stumbled, or if I had really fallen over a cliff. It seemed more likely that I had stumbled. The rock wall that had barred my passage might indeed be the rock beside me. The sights and the smells and the sounds of the night were most likely the sounds produced by the juices of the plants I had chewed. But what about the pain? Could peyote or loco weed leave a body so wracked with pain?

One by one, I carefully moved each arm and leg, searchin' for broken bones. The movements brought neither increase nor decrease in the pain. And everything seemed to be workin'. I rolled over and managed to get hands and knees under me. The effort cost me. The ground under me suddenly began to spin, carryin' me with it. And then the earth was still and the sky was spinnin'. I closed my eyes and let my head hang. I wouldn't lay back down. My next move had to be to my feet. My own ragged breathin' filled the canyon like the roar of the wind. As the wind eventually lays, so my breathin' finally steadied. The poundin' from within my chest faded and died and still I was on my knees.

Silence filled the canyons. My ears strained for the sounds they had heard, yet had not. The sound was so familiar I couldn't mistake it, and so out of place I couldn't believe it. When it came again the hair raised on the back of my neck. There was nothing fearful about the sound itself. It was the time and the place that made me even notice the snorting of the horse.

"It could be a wild horse," I told myself. "Yeah, and everybody that believes that can suck an egg." It didn't seem any stranger to answer myself than it did to open the conversation.

I forced my feet to take my weight and only slightly staggered as I moved toward the sound. Silently, I begged the empty night for a repeat of the sound. Nothing. Then a short bleatin' sound like a sheep. Or goat. Could it have been a goat snortin'? Bein' truthful with myself, I had to admit I had never heard a goat snort. But I had heard the sound a thousand times before and would bet my life it was a horse. I might be bettin' more than my own life. I couldn't forget Annie.

The smell brought me up short. It was smoke. Not the smoke of a fire, but the lingering smoke of a cedar knot spittin' its oil onto the coals of a fire gone nearly dead. Somewhere out in the darkness, there was a camp. A camp made by a man unafraid to build a fire in Indian country, a camp with at least one horse and a goat. It might be a sheep. And a woman! The sounds in the night. The Angel singin'. It had to be a woman. And the odds were, the woman was Annie Baxter. But singin'?

Carefully, I dropped to my knees and began to crawl. The moonlight was strong enough to let me see to walk, but I couldn't trust my own body. I might fall or step on a twig or send a rock rollin' to warn of my comin'. Inch by eternal inch, I made my way toward the enemy.

My probin' fingers sifted the sand and cleared debris from the rocky ground. But I couldn't clear away all the thousands of pea-sized rocks and gravel that ground into my knees. Each time my weight rested on my knees, the pain drove me so close to a grunt or oath that I had to force my mind to hold onto the vision of Annie to drive my body on.

The fire wasn't dead. The cedar knot spilled its sap among the hot coals. Tongues of flame licked the night air ever so gently and left their glow to light the tiny hollow. My strainin' eyes traced the outline of the woman as she sat asleep. Her back was against the rock wall. Her feet were tucked under her and her knees were close to the fire. Like a saint deep in prayer, her chin lay on her breast. Her arms held a bundle without size or shape. At the time I never gave it a thought, but later I knew she held a baby. Maybe it was the protective way she held the bundle, even in her sleep.

I wanted to believe it was Annie, but there was no light to see the turned-up nose or the twinkle in her eye, the youthful strength, nor the perfect proportions of her body.

The man lay asleep beside the fire. At least he looked to me to be asleep. It's hard to figure how a sleepin' man could explode into action like he did, though. The rupper part of his body was covered by a blanket or robe. The moccasins of the Commanche warrior covered his feet.

There were no horses in the little hollow. But they would be picketed on grass near by. The only creature awake in the camp was the nanny goat. She looked me in the eye as I brought my revolver from its holster and aimed it at the sleepin' Indian.

I've got to confess, I don't honestly know whether I would have shot him in his sleep or not. I was strugglin' with the thought of walkin' in and tryin' to take him prisoner, but I realized my weakness. If anything went wrong, I might die and leave Annie in the hands of the Other One. But to just shoot him in the dark

67

like he was nothing? Maybe I could have if I had hated him. But somehow it seemed every encounter I had with the Indian made my respect for him grow. And it's hard to work up much of a hate for a man you respect.

My thumb found its familiar place on the hammer of the Colt. The hammer clicked as it came back and the cylinder click-clicked as the next round rolled into position. The sound was hardly more than a whisper, but it was enough. Too much.

The hollow went blacker than the darkest pitch as the Indian's robe covered the tiny fire. I cursed myself for the fool I had been, starin' into the light so long. I could almost see the sounds as the Other One drove his camp before him. The woman screamed and the goat bleated as they were forced over the rim of the hollow. The grunts of the Indian and the sound of a fist on flesh quieted the woman and the goat. I wondered which he had struck. I strained for the sounds of horses' hoofs on rock, but there was only the roar of total silence.

8

Massacre

"This is as far as the trail goes."

The speaker was the big Preacher who had appointed himself leader of the posse. He stood beside the black man whose tracking skills had kept them on the trail so far. For half a day the posse had circled the flock of sheep. The sheep tracks totally obliterated the tracks left by the Indian and the girl.

"They probably left on foot," someone said.

"Yeah, and what did they do with their horses? Eat them?" A second voice ridiculed the first speaker.

"Besides," Joe Baxter said, "even if the Indian could disappear on foot, he couldn't take Annie with him."

From someone in the midst of the posse a callous voice said, "Hell, she's probably dead and buried somewhere under all these tracks."

An awkward silence followed the remark as the posse waited to see the effect it had on Joe Baxter. It was soon evident the possibility had not escaped Joe. He gave no outward sign of having heard the remark. "Could he be following the horses on foot, erasing the tracks?" The question was aimed at Estavan.

"No." The negative answer was emphatic. "Once a track is made, it can't be hidden, except by something like a hundred sheep wiping it out. Even on solid rock the scratch of a horseshoe is like nothing else. To try to erase it leaves a mark easier to see than the track itself. There just ain't no tracks here.''

"Well, they didn't fly away. How do you figure they got away without leaving tracks?" Estavan had no answer for the question. A thousand times in the hours since he lost the tracks, he had asked himself the same question.

"I wish I had an answer. Without the answer to that question, we may never find the girl.''

"Hell, nigger, you know as well as the rest of us, we ain't never gonna find that girl.''

Estavan's eyes searched the posse for the man who had made the statement. They all looked guilty, and they probably all felt the same way. Knowing the other girl, Irene Tucker, and what Indian captivity had done to her, most of the men secretely hoped they wouldn't find Annie. To find the Indian who had taken her and take revenge upon him would be enough.

"We'll find her," Joe Baxter shouted. "And she'll be all right! She won't be like Irene.'' The words were loud with anger, but weak like those of a politician who knows he has lost the election, but isn't ready to admit it. Down deep inside, Joe Baxter was sure he had lost his sister.

Trying to regain leadership of the group, Preacher said, "All right, if they didn't ride out of here, then the horses are still here somewhere. It's for sure they couldn't dig a hole big enough to bury them in. If they're here, we'll find them in a creek someplace with the bank caved in on them.''

"I seen a place like that," Joe said, showing new signs of life. "About a quarter mile over east. The ground was soft like it had been dug recently. And there was a thousand sheep tracks through it.''

70

As one body, the posse moved toward the place Joe spoke of. "Get some shovels from the wagon," Preacher commanded.

Without argument, two of the younger men rode at a lope to the wagon. They quickly returned with the shovels and began the digging. The bones they uncovered were far too small to be from horses, and the anxiety of the men made them fear the worst. They know of no cannibals among the Plains Indians, but then, they knew less than they liked to admit about any Indians.

The pile of bones grew until finally one allowed his reason to penatrate his fears. "Hell," he said, "they're sheep. They're sheep bones."

For the first time since the first bone was uncovered, there was almost a light-heartedness among the men. "At least that redskin's eatin' good," said one man. "He must have killed half a dozen sheep. Cleaned their bones slick as a whistle."

"Wonder what he did with the hides?" someone else questioned.

A look of understanding crossed the face of Estavan. Without a word, he walked out among the flock and caught a young ram. He deftly slit the animal's throat.

"What's the matter with you?" Joe Baxter asked. "We don't have to eat that stinkin' mutton just because the Indian is. We've got plenty of beef and bacon on the wagon."

Estavan didn't bother to answer. He quickly skinned the animal and cut the skin into four pieces. He tied a piece over each hoof of the mule he rode. As if by magic, the posse watched the tracks become nothing but smudges in the soft dirt, like where a wind-blown weed had passed.

The Indian had led them on a south-by-southwest

71

course from the start. It seemed obvious to most of the men that he was headed toward Mexico.

"I ain't sayin' we ought to stop when we get to the Rio Grande," someone said, "but I sure hope we don't have to go no farther than that. Them Mexicans sure would like an excuse to send soldiers back into Texas."

"Send soldiers, hell. If we get down there and get caught, we ain't comin' back. Them Mex soldiers would rather get hold of us than a bunch of redskins anyday."

Night camp was a time when the leaders of the posse gathered to plan the next day's march. So far it had been little more than a session for keeping inventory of supplies and check on livestock condition. For the first time, the night after the trail was lost brought dissension among the men.

"I want to know why we've been veerin' so much west?" The speaker was Henry Tucker. "Ever since we left the settlements, that redskin's been headin' more south than anything. How come you all of a sudden figure he turned west?"

Estavan started to answer, but Preacher cut him off. "We figure the Indian to be Comanche. He'll be goin' to his people. This time of year the Comanche will be on the Llano followin' the buffalo north."

"If he's Comanche and figgerin' on goin' north, how come he lit out south toward Mexico?"

"If you was bein' chased by twenty men, would you be anxious for them to know where you was headed?"

Anger reddened the face of Tucker. "You sayin' I ain't smart enough to follow that Indian?"

"O' course not, Henry." The Preacher tried to soothe the feelings of the other man. "It's just that me and Estavan have been talkin' this over and figure the

72

reason the Comanche suddenly decided to hide his tracks was cause he was fixin' to change directions.''

"What makes you so damm sure it's a Comanche that got the girl? I reckon I know about as much as anybody about the different tribes, and I ain't seen a thing to make me believe it's any more likely he was Comanche than anything else.''

Preacher searched his mind for an answer to the question. What was it? The way he set the ambush? The way he hid his tracks? The direction he took? Tucker was right. There was nothing that said Comanche except his gut feeling. And that of Estavan. They had fought the Comanche on the Llano beside Laliker. When a man fights and survives, he recognizes his enemy when they fight again. The enemy was Comanche—but what evidence could he show Tucker?

The silence answered Tucker's question. The man seized the opportunity to grasp at leadership of the posse. To the whole group he shouted, "I don't know why, but we're bein' led off on some kind of goose-hunt. It's plain as the nose on your face, that redskin's headin' for Mexico. It don't take a real bright redskin to know the Mexicans ain't gonna stand for a posse of gringos crossin' the Rio. I say we turn south and double-time it to make up for the day we lost!''

The cold eyes of Tucker searched the posse for support. They first picked out Wilson. The man cringed before the consuming hatred he saw in those eyes. Because he so feared the man, he took Tucker's side of the argument. "Tucker's right. You all know what it cost him when we let the redskins that took Irene get a head start. I say we push south as hard and fast and far as we have too to find the girl.''

A murmur of agreement went through the group. Tucker was quick to push his advantage. "The

73

Preacher and the nigger was off on the Llano last year when the Indians took my Irene. They had a run-in with a few Comanches and got the idea all Indian troubles are caused by the Comanches. It wasn't Comanches that took my Irene, and I don't see any reason to think it was Comanches that got little Annie. There ain't been a Comanche anywhere near Denton County in years.''

The excited arguments kindled the fantasies of young Bob Cooley. Following the Preacher had brought him no closer to the chance to live out his dreams of rescuing the girl and winning her love. For the first time in his life, he stood up and shouted to be heard. He seemed to forget the nasal twang of his voice as he stepped from the fantasy world into the drama of the moment. ''I go with Tucker! The Comanches ain't never done nothin' to us. We ain't got no reason to ride out to that God-forsaken place huntin' more Indian trouble than we already got. I say we head south and try to cut them off at the border.''

For Cooley it was a speech of major proportions. The mere fact that he had opened his mouth among so many was enough to win many nods of agreement. It also left a silence that allowed the soft voice of Manuel Ortiz to be heard. ''Have not Tucker and Wilson reasons to lead us on a vengeful trail of striking at any red men we see? Surely you have all heard the stories of evil laid at the door of Tucker. Would you have such a man lead you? Always the Preacher has guided as well. I see no reason to turn against him now.''

Tucker was enraged. ''We've all heard those lies and we all know there ain't a bit of truth in them!'' Turning his eyes from the man to the crowd, he continued. ''It's clear why Ortiz don't want to head south. Them greasers ain't never give in to the idea that Texas

74

belongs to the white men. He don't want to see none of his Mexican friends get stepped on if they get in our way. I say it would be a good idea to run him and a bunch of others back to Mexico where they belong!''

The calm voice of Ortiz demanded as much attention as Tucker's tirade. "My family has lived on Texas soil for a hundred years. I was born in Texas and my parents were born in Texas. And I have children born in Texas. I followed Sam Houston to San Jacento and saw my own brother die to make Texas free. I had two cousins in the Alamo with Colonel Travis. Where were you when this happened? I don't remember you at San Jacento and surely you were not at the Alamo.''

Tucker quickly retreated from the sacred ground his words had led him onto. "I say we split the posse. Let Preacher and whoever else figures he's right head west. The rest of us can take the supply wagon and push south. We can double our chances of catchin' that redskin.''

"Fair enough," Preacher surprised Tucker with his quick agreement to the plan. "I'll be honest enough to tell you I got nothin but a gut feelin' about our Indian bein' a Comanche and him headin' west. I do agree with Tucker that we've lost the whole day. We're gonna have to push mighty hard to cut them off whether they headed south or west.''

"I'll ride with Preacher," Joe Baxter cast his vote of confidence in the Preacher's judgement. "It don't make sense to me for the Indian to lay a trail a kid could follow, then suddenly decide to hide his tracks unless he had a trick up his sleeve.''

"Yeah, and the trick might be that he ain't changin' direction at all." Tucker's logic was as reasonable as any other.

"I say we ride with Tucker." The new speaker was Wilson. "There ain't a man alive knows more than him about the ways of Indians. If his hunch says south, then I'm for goin' south.''

"Me, too," young Bob Cooley cut in. "Killin' redskins ain't no job for preachers and niggers anyway. They'd want to have sangin' and preachin' and dinner on the ground if we caught them murderin' devils.''

The lines were drawn. Only Estavan and Joe Baxter would ride west with the Preacher. It was good. A small group could survive better on the limited water supplies on the Llano than a large group could. Preacher was disappointed that Ortiz had not joined him. The Mexican's explanation could not be denied, though.

"I must ride with Tucker. His hate of the red man has burned out his soul. He will soon be killing anyone whose skin is dark and whose hair is coarse and black. Before he starts killing Mexicans, I will shoot him down for the mad dog he is becoming.''

Before noon the next day, Tucker picked up the tracks. Two horses headed South. Estavan could have told them the tracks were not made by the horses they followed from the settlements. And he could have told them the riders were hunters, not men fleeing from an angry posse. But Estavan was not with them. He was with Preacher and Joe Baxter heading west toward the Llano.

The tracks led the posse to the camp.

"Kiowa," Tucker said. "I knew Preacher was full of bull about it bein' Comanches. If that Baxter girl's alive, she'd down there in that camp.''

"How do you figure to get her out?" The question came from Wilson.

"I don't know but one way to deal with Indians. We ride in and shoot them down Dead squaws and papooses is a language them bucks understand.''

"You're talking massacre!" The look of shocked

horror on the face of Ortiz said he would have no part of Tucker's plan.

"Call it what ever you want to. What was it when them Indians killed Wilson's boy and done what they did to my Irene? There ain't a white man or woman or child safe in this cuntry as long as there's a single redskin breathin'."

The hate of Tucker was a vile and infectious thing. It was a disease, spreading its evil into the hearts and souls of the posse. The group became an animal and the animal turned upon the last semblance of reason within it.

"You're a halfbreed, Ortiz." Tucker spoke for the posse. "You've done nothin' since we left the settlements but whine about the poor Indians bein' mistreated. I've heard all I aim to from you."

"Will you kill me to shut me up?"

The question was a challenge. It took all of Tucker's reason and strength to overcome the desire to shoot the man off his horse. There were too many witnesses. And too many Indians. The Kiowa camp was just over a little rise. A shot would warn them and he would be cheated out of his chance to kill.

"No, I won't kill you, unless you make me. But hear me good, Mex. You do anything, anything at all, to warn those Indians we're here, and I'll draw and quarter you."

The attack came out of the setting sun. Thirty Kiowa braves stood between the fury that descended upon them and their women and children. The guns of the white men knew no difference between brave and squaw, no difference between aged and infant. Five minutes of hell left forty Kiowa dead or dying in the sand—forty Kiowa and Manuel Ortiz.

When the white men were gone, the Kiowa came

again. Those who had escaped into the brush gathered their dead. The women wept and the men swore vengeance. The children looked upon the carnage and learned well their lessons in hate and murder and savagery.

They gathered their belongings and headed to the north and west, toward the Llano where there were plenty of buffalo. There the enemy was the Comanche and there were no white men. The white men couldn't seem to understand the game. The game was to steal the horses and women and even the children of the enemy. All the white man wanted or understood was to kill.

The grief of the Kiowa blinded their eyes. None saw the two white men separate themselves from the others. They saw neither the shame and guilt in the faces of the larger group, nor the insatiable hate and lust in the eyes of the two.

When the Kiowa left the place of sorrow, death followed them. The slow-witted Bob Cooley had found the fulfillment of his dreams. With his gun in hand and defenseless people before him, he became the sword of vengeance he dreamed himself to be. With the cunning insanity of Henry Tucker to lead him, he would never again be laughed at, or ignored.

9

The Gathering of Forces

"How do you figure it?"

Two days north and west of where they left the posse, they found the tracks. Estavan's answer was as Preacher expected. "It was a freight wagon. A big one, too, I figure. From the size of it, it would have to be one of Laliker's."

"You don't think he's with the wagon?"

"No, he's probably got some men two or three days ahead of the wagon. Probably has pack horses and just brought the wagon along in case the trail runs too long."

"How long since they passed?"

"Can't say for sure. Could have been any time in the last couple of days. There ain't much out here to disturb tracks."

"Who's this feller Laliker?"

The pair of giants had almost forgotten the younger man. "You met him at the picnic," Preacher answered. "He's the gent with the Tennessee rifle that won all the marbles in the turkey shoot."

"Why would he be out here?"

"I reckon you was too busy steamin' over gettin' beat to notice the shine he took to your sister."

"I noticed. But what would make him head this

direction? Why wouldn't he have joined the posse and followed them like the rest of us?''

"Laliker ain't like the rest of us. Me an' Estavan have had a feelin' from the start about this bein Comanche work. It looks like somethin' gave Laliker that same feelin'. Or maybe it was more than a feelin'. Maybe there was somethin' there that said 'Comanche' big and bold and Laliker was the only one that could read it. Whatever the reason, the point is, he bet it all on whatever told him to head west. He didn't waste a day headin' south. Chances are, he beat the Comanche to the caprock by at least two days.''

It takes a strong horse to carry a big man day after day. Preacher longed for the roan animal that had brought him to Texas. The gait of the animal was as smooth as flowing water and the broad back was a more comfortable seat than most stuffed chairs. But as fine as the animal was, it couldn't have kept pace with the mule he rode. Mile after endless mile, the pounding, jarring, step of the mule shook him till he feared his joints would come apart and his teeth would fall out. There seemed no end to the everlasting miles the almost tireless mules carried their burdens in the race ever westward. Joe Baxter was hard put to keep up, even though he changed horses twice a day.

Night camps were late in coming. As long as there was light, the two giants pushed their animals. Four hours of total dark forced them to rest a short time each night. But when the moon again showed the wagon tracks, they drove themselves and their stock further west. By the third noon, even the mules had tired to the point of faltering. Preacher and Estavan knew it was only a matter of time before the animals would balk. A good horse will die under a rider. He will go until his heart breaks and he dies. No such

80

thing for a mule. When he has gone his limit, he will balk and no power on earth can make him take another step.

Preacher gambled on overtaking the wagon before the mules balked. It became more evident as the miles went by that he had bet on a loser. Though the tracks seemed fresher, the wagon might still be hours ahead of them.

"Look for a place to make camp," Preacher said. "My mule is figgerin' on balkin' on me."

"I remember this place," Estavan answered. "Over this next hill there is a stream. The grass is good and we can rest through the night."

"How far are we from the caprock?"

"Half a day. Less on fresh mules."

"Will we be able to get on top somewhere close to here?"

"We're a ways north of the place we took the wagons up last summer. We may have to drop back south a little when we get to the cap."

"That's where you first ran into the Comanches, ain't it?"

"Right," Estavan re-told the story. "We was just about to top out when they attacked us. Laliker killed a half-dozen with that Colt of his and scared the devil out of twice that many more. He swears his horse ran away with him and he didn't have any choice but to shoot Comanches or die. 'Maybe so,' I told him, 'but it wasn't no runaway horse that aimed his Colt and sent an Indian to his reward everytime the pistol fired.' And him twistin' and jerkin' and goin' every which way right in the middle of that whole band of redskins. And all the while there wasn't a bullet or arrow or knife touched him."

"Yeah," Preacher agreed. "You can't blame the Comanches for figurin' he was bad medicine and settin' their best man on him. By their way of thinkin', I expect every bit of bad luck they've had since that day was Laliker's fault.''

The conversation brought them to the top of the hill. It was just like Estavan had described it. The grass was tall and green and the stream ran clear and cold. Only one thing was different. The grass was spotted with mules and saddle horses and the freight wagon was camped beside the stream.

Their arrival in the camp was welcomed by the cook, Sam. "Preacher, Estavan!" he named them as he shook their hands. "Don't reckon I've met you," he said as he turned to reach for the younger man's hand.

"Joe Baxter."

"You'd be the brother of the girl, Annie?"

"That's right."

"Well, maybe I have some news for you." The older man paused long enough to stir the anxiety in his audience to a fever pitch. Just as Preacher was about to demand that he get on with it, he started his story.

"It was day before yesterday, O'Leary and Dominguez come a leadin' Laliker into camp. He was in bad shape, sufferin' mostly from thirst. He had found himself some water, but his body was so dried up, he was a long way from havin' his full strength. Anyway, he said he spotted the Comanche and the girl just before dawn that same mornin'. They was camped in a wash up close to the top of the cap. He figured both of them to be asleep, but when he cocked his pistol all hell broke loose. The Indian threw his robe over the fire and snaked the woman and baby out of there before Laliker could so much as say howdy.''

"Baby?" The questioning word burst from three mouths at the same time.

82

"Sure. The girl had a baby. It was her a-singin' lullabies to it that led Laliker to their camp. You fellers didn't hear of a baby bein' kidnapped, too, did you?"

"No, but that explains the cradle board and wrappings we found," Estavan said. "The baby must belong to the Indian. But how could it survive the kind of push they would have been doing?"

"Laliker said there was a goat."

"Sure," Estavan said. "A nanny goat. Stolen from the flock of sheep."

"How long since Laliker and the others left?" The question came from the anxious Joe Baxter.

"First light this mornin'. They're goin' to try to pick up the Indian's tracks. Only there wasn't any close to the spring. Laliker said they must have flown in there and out again, for all the tracks their horses left."

Estavan told the cook how the Comanche had used the sheep skins to hide their tracks and lose the posse. "He must have kept some hides back for the same purpose here."

The others agreed with Estavan's reasoning.

"Are you going to try to follow them?" Preacher asked the cook.

"No, too much chance of gettin' off the trail on the Llano. If they run out of supplies, they can always find me here. If I was to get lost out there and they needed me, they could starve to death a mile from the wagon."

"Will you spare us mules and horses to go on, then?"

"You know you don't have to ask. Take your pick. Watch out for that blue Jack, though. He's meaner than a Comanche. There ain't no way I'd walk up to him without a doubletree in my hand to show him who's boss."

83

The trio easily picked up the tracks of Laliker and the others. A day's head start was not much, figuring the ease of following men who had no reason to hide their tracks, compared with the almost impossible tracking chore laid out by the Indian.

It was late on the third day before they heard the shot. Sounds carried forever on the Llano, but not with the authority of the sound they heard. It came from just over the rise ahead of them.

There was no need for commands or discussion among the three. Even young Joe Baxter had lived long enough in the savage land to instinctively drop from his mount. Estavan and Baxter spread wide to nearly circle the hill before Preacher slipped to the top.

The scene spread before Preacher was the drama of life and death that was a continual part of frontier survival. The eyes of the Mexican, Dominguez, were methodically searching for the Indian he knew was somewhere near. Occasionally he paused in his search to fire a revolver shot into a more likely hiding place. In time the Mexican's searching eyes would complete their circle and find the Indian sneaking up behind him. But there was no time. A few more feet would put him close enough for a lunge with the knife he held.

Preacher took careful aim at the Indian's head. His finger squeezed the trigger ever so gently. Half a breath of life was all that was left for the Other One. Who can say whether it was compassion bred from his religious beliefs, or a decision to take the man alive that caused the muzzle of the rifle to veer ever so slightly from its target in the split second of the falling of the hammer.

10

The Man-Animals

Like wolves on the scent of a flock of sheep, Tucker and Cooley followed the Kiowa people westward. One Indian, or two, could easily hide their tracks. Even a war party of ten or twelve could make a tracker labor to stay on their trail. But a tribe on the move, by its very nature, literally cut a path upon the plains. The hoofs of the many horses cut the turf and left the ground open and raw. The travois upon which the women carried the possessions of the tribe cut twin furrows in the earth. Tucker and Cooley followed in the wake of the tribe.

For several days, they hung well back to keep the Indians from discovering their presence. They followed their prey across the scrub oak and mesquite lands and to the caprock that lifted the Llano Estacado high above the near ground. Over the caprock and out onto the Llano they followed, into the land of the Comanche and the Kiowa. The air was so clear the miles shrank to yards. A man could see farther than he could ride in a day on a good horse.

Tucker and Cooley saw all these things, but they didn't see the arroyos that cut the land like some giant hand had gouged out trenches with a stick. Nor did they see the playa lakes that dimpled the land and held in their bottoms the precious water that sustained life on the Llano.

The moon lit the land like a great lantern. Two nights from the caprock, Tucker could wait no longer. The blood lust inside him rose like gorge in his throat and had to be satisfied.

Bob Cooley watched as his mentor transformed himself before his eyes. From somewhere in his pack, Tucker produced the clothing of a Kiowa brave. From moccasins to headdress, he became a Kiowa.

"Where did you get them Injun clothes?" Cooley asked, after the change was nearly complete.

"Hell. I took 'em off a dead Injun. Where the hell you think I got 'em?"

"When? I've been with you all the time and I never seen you kill no Injun."

"How stupid can one man get? I've had these ever since we butchered that bunch when we was with the posse."

"I never seen you takin' no clothes off no Injun that night."

"There were a lot of things happened that night that nobody saw."

"Yeah? Like what?"

"Like that smart-mouth Mex Ortiz gittin' the top of his head blowed off."

"Do you mean you was the one that killed Ortiz?"

"What the hell did you think I meant?"

"But he was a white man."

"White, hell. Them Mexicans is all more Injun than white. Did you ever see anybody but a greaser with hair and eyes that black? Anybody but an Injun, that is."

"I know they're part Injun. But Ortiz was on our side."

"The hell he was. He never fired a shot. He just

set there on his horse watchin' it all and makin' them signs touchin' his head and sholders and belly. And all the time he was mumbling somethin' in Mex about Mother of God and sweet Jesus."

"I liked Ortiz. He never made fun of me and he took me fishin' lots."

"Well, you wouldn't have liked him if he had got back to the settlements. Anybody with any sense could see he figured on goin' straight to the army with his stories about us wipin' out those redskins."

"So what? The army kills redskins."

"Not without orders, they don't. They figure if soldiers is told to go out and wipe out a whole tribe, it's okay. They're just followin' the orders of the generals and politicians. But if civilians kill a few Injuns to make life safe for their women, then that's murder and a body that does it is likely to get himself hung."

"Aw, they wouldn't."

"The hell they wouldn't. There was three men hung six or eight months ago up at Fort Gibson just for killin' a dozen or so redskins that was campin' on their land and eatin' their beef."

"No!"

"Hell, yes! They hung 'em just like they was murderers or somethin'."

"I still liked Mr. Ortiz."

"Damm! Ain't you got it through your thick head? It was him or us. If he ever told the army what he seen, we would be hung higher than a two week drunk."

"Well, watcha got them Injun clothes on for? You ain't gonna make no Injun think you're one of them."

"You're so stupid, I don't know whether you can understand or not. It ain't the Injuns I aim to fool. I ain't never seen the Injun I couldn't sneak up on just about as close as I want to get."

"Well, hell. There ain't nobody else out here to fool, except me. And I already know you ain't no Injun."

"There's the dogs, stupid. If you didn't stink so bad yourself, you'd know there's a difference in the smell of a white man and an Injun. Them Injun dogs would raise so much hell I couldn't get in a hundred yards of that camp if I tried to sneak in smellin' like a white man. But they're so used to smellin' the stink of the Injuns they won't pay no attention to me with these clothes on."

"I don't stink that bad."

"Just don't never let your nose get downwind from your body, and you might go on thinkin' that."

Tucker spurred his horse and left Cooley to puzzle out his last words. "That stupid kid's liable to get me killed," he thought. "But he does like killin' Injuns and it might be good to have my back covered if I stir up more than I can handle."

A mile or more from the Kiowa camp, Tucker left his horse tied to a mesquite bush. The bright glow of the moon flooded the ground and left Tucker feeling naked, exposed to every probing eye. Yet, who would be watchin? Days and miles lay between the Kiowa and the dreaded place of death that came from the glare of the setting sun. Tucker was sure the Indians knew nothing of the two who followed them. If they knew, they would surely have left a trap, or turned to fight.

A quarter mile from the camp, Tucker could see movement among the tepees. A few Indian women still tended the fires and a few men stood with their backs to the fires, staring into the surrounding darkness.

The hunter kept a low hill to his back as he drew near the camp. It would not do to skyline himself and alert the prey. Two hundred yards from the camp, he dropped to his knees and studied the enemy. The blood lust inside him drove him to hurry, to fall upon his enemy and kill.

But the cunning in his brain told him to go carefully. Many times since his daughter, Irene, fell victim to the Indian attack, he faced similar situations. Always he managed to capture or kill his prey. But never before did he have a chance at a whole tribe. The taste of revenge and insane hatred was bittersweet in his mouth. "How many?" he asked himself. Could he kill ten? or twenty? Like a great cat he moved silently, stealthily, on toward the camp. His rifle lay beside a bush, primed and ready to be grabbed for a quick shot in case he was forced to leave the camp in a hurry. It made little difference that he probably couldn't find the rifle again if the need arose. The weapon was too cumbersome to carry further. The work he had laid out for himself was knife work. Silent work. He wanted to feel the flesh of the Indians part under the edge of his blade. He wanted to feel the vengeance for his daughter flow on his hands.

The Indian sentry stood only a few feet away. Desperately, Tucker fought the urge to lunge recklessly to grab the man. The alarm must not be sounded. This one must die quietly, for Tucker knew he could not be satisfied to take only one life that night. The kill fever was too high in him. He would kill many, even if it meant dying himself. And Tucker had no intention of dying. As long as there was another victim for his knife, another chance to feel the blood flowing on his hands, he would not surrender his life.

Across the camp a dog barked. The Indian turned and Tucker struck. As swiftly as a snake, his left hand covered the mouth and nose of his victum. The razor-sharp point of the knife hesitated a second before it slipped between the ribs of the Indian.

"Know you're dead," Tucker whispered into the ear. "Think about every time you laid your filthy hands on a decent woman. And ask yourself if it was worth it."

It made no difference that the Indian probably didn't understand a word he spoke. And it made no difference that the Indian whose life he held had probably never touched a white woman. The revenge was for Irene. And the blood that gushed forth was the blood of all the hated Indians.

Tucker held the body until it quit jerking. Even before the final twitch, his eyes were searching for his next victim.

He paused at the entrance to the tepee. From inside, he could hear the deep breathing of several people. There was nothing to indicate any were awake. Quietly he slipped through the open doorway and moved to the back of the lodge. His heart beat like a drum, and it seemed it must surely awaken the people in the tent. Gradually his eyes adjusted to the dim light of the moon that found its way through the open doorway and through the smoke hole in the top of the tepee.

Disappointment filled Tucker. There were only three. A young couple lay side by side. Their child of only two or three years slept across the lodge on a robe of its own.

"First the man," Tucker told himself. "Then the woman."

His hand fell across the face of the woman at the same instant his knife plunged into the throat of the sleeping man. The sounds made by the man died in a gurgle as the blood from the severed jugular rushed into the open air passage. In the seconds while he died, the brave watched the same knife that had killed him

90

plunge into the breast of his woman. He had strength left to hate the invader, but no strength to strike at his murderer. Death kept him from being forced to watch as the knife plunged into the tiny body across the tepee.

The dog sniffed at the blood-smeared figure that emerged from the tepee. The half-wild animal drew back on his haunches and bared his teeth. A long, low growl started somewhere deep inside the animal and made its way to the air. Tucker cursed as the beast lunged at him.

The knife ripped the dog's shoulder open and sent him yelping across the camp. Tucker ran, knife in hand, toward the hill which had covered his approach to the camp. A dozen dogs barked in pursuit of the fleeing figure.

The dogs brought their quarry to the ground a hundred yards from the outer edge of the camp. Tucker came up, slashing and stabbing with his knife. The yelps of wounded dogs drove the pack back long enough for the man to get his revolver from its holster. Two shots into the midst of the pack sent all the animals yelping for the protection of their masters.

A quick search failed to produce the rifle Tucker left hidden in the tall grass. Disgusted at the loss, but glad to be away from the dogs, the man went in search of his horse.

The evidence was clear. He was in the right place. The ground was churned up with the tracks. There was the mesquite bush where he had left the animal tied, and the close-nipped grass where the horse grazed while he waited for the man to return. But there was no horse.

Bob Cooley heard the distant shots. Instantly he sprang to his feet and threw the saddle on his horse. Shots meant trouble for Tucker. Cooley had quenched his own blood-thirst often on the intoxicating stories

Tucker told. He knew Tucker would use his knife for the night's work. Only the worst imaginable trouble could make the man go to his revolver. Cooley rode into the night to help the one he considered his friend.

The bark of dogs and yip of coyotes hung in the night air. But Bob Cooley listened for other sounds. Somewhere Tucker was in trouble. Cooley listened for the sound of a voice calling to him. He listened for the approach of running feet. And his eyes searched the moonlit prairie for any sign of life. All was still except the owl that flew up in his face and caused him to grab for his revolver, only to shove it back in embarrassment.

Tucker walked toward the camp where he had left Cooley. His only regret was that with only one horse, they would have to turn back. It would be foolish to follow the Indians farther. They were aware of his presence and would search him out. The plan had been to strike at the Indians, back off for a few days, then hit them again. But one horse was not enough. They would have to walk most of the way back to the settlements. And there would always be another Indian to kill.

The sound broke through the man's thoughts. A horse. Coming toward him. Silently, Tucker dropped to the earth. The tall grass hid him from any viewer. He listened breathlessly while the horse brought its burden ever closer. The animal was almost directly over him when he burst from his hiding place, knife in hand. The blood-hungry blade swung its arc while Tucker sprang at the rider. The knife sank to the hilt in Bob Cooley's chest.

Tucker looked at what he had done and shrugged his shoulders. "I left the fool in camp. If he had done what I told him, he wouldn't have got hisself killed."

The words floated unheard across the grassland, but they left Tucker fully satisfied he had done no wrong.

The horse backed away from the blood-spattered figure. The more Tucker coaxed, the wilder the animal became. Finally Tucker made a lunge at the animal and sent it in a panicked run straight toward the Kiowa camp. Tucker turned and started the long walk to Texas.

11

Face to Face

I cursed myself for being so stupid. Even a greenhorn would have known better than to cock his gun before he had the target dead to rights. Sure, I could have killed the Indian. I could have shot the whole camp to pieces. But shootin' her wasn't exactly the plans I had for Annie Baxter.

My eyes adjusted to the darkness of the washout. Occasionally I could see the moonlight reflect off the water from the spring. And I could hear its splash as it made its way downward toward the thousands of mostly dry creeks and riverbeds that cut the land below the cap into a maze of hills and valleys.

The shining reflections were like the seductive call of a woman as she silently offers herself to her lover. The rippling sounds of the water fallin' pulled at me just as the legendary siren songs pulled at sea-goin' men for ages. Songs leading men to their deaths.

For several hours, or maybe it was just a few minutes, I resisted the call of the water. The Other One probably lay out there somewhere waiting for me to make a move. I argued with myself that even though the Indian might remain motionless and totally quiet for an unending time, the woman and the goat and the child wouldn't. But the argument didn't hold much water when faced with the sure knowledge that the Indian would kill all of them without hesitation if he thought it would buy him a chance at me.

Like I said, I don't know if hours or minutes had passed before I decided to take my chances. I might die if there was a trap set, but I would surely die without the water. My body said it couldn't wait 'til daylight, but my brain didn't give in 'til it remembered how the Other One hid in our camp on the Llano and had only accidently been found by Estavan. Even when the light came, I might not be able to tell if the Indian was gone. So be it, I decided. The Indian might kill me, but I wouldn't die of thirst thirty feet from a flowing spring.

The Indian was gone. The water was cool and sweet. I drank and I slept.

I took the easier way around the bottom of the cap going back for my horses and supplies. I was bitter disappointed at the failure of my trap, but I at least had the knowledge that Annie was still alive. I had bet my whole roll on beatin' the Indian to the Llano and settin' my trap for him. Now I had nothin' left but to follow him out onto the plains, expectin' at each moment for him to raise up out of the ground or shoot me from ambush. There was no way to find him. All I could do was wait, and hope I was ready when he came.

Halfway back to the draw, I met O'Leary and Dominguez. They had my horses and supplies and they had water. I argued the point, but couldn't even convince myself that I needed to go on after Annie immediately. O'Leary made a lot of sense in his arguments.

"Let him wonder. He thinks he heard somethin'. He'll be expectin' you to come chargin' after him like somethin' out of the night. Chances are, he's got a trap laid for you right now. Let him stew in his own trap. By night he'll figure the noise he heard was nothin' but a dream. Give him the rest of today and tomorrow and he'll convince himself there never was a noise. He's liable to turn around and head back into our arms.''

I'm not sure whether I came to agree with O'Leary's logic or whether my body's demand for rest convinced me, but eventually I gave up the argument and went back to the wagon with the men.

A man ain't given to look into the future. All he can do is make a decision based on the knowledge he has and stick by it. If I could have seen the things ahead, I might have rushed out after Annie the minute I had a horse under me. 'Course, if I could see into the future, I would have known whether or not I would have been in time to do any good or not anyway. When I decided to rest a day, I did it with an easy mind, knowin' I would need to be at the peak of my strength of body and mind when I met the Other One again. The only thing I was sure of was that I would meet him.

There wasn't a sign of tracks anywhere near the spring in the wash where I had spooked the Indian. No tracks but my own and the few footprints around the spring itself. Of course the goat had cut a few tracks, but there were no horse tracks.

We had no reason to figure the Other One would head anywhere except onto the Llano, so we made our way to the top. I sent O'Leary right and Dominguez left and took the middle for myself. ''Sooner or later his horses are gonna cut tracks,'' I told them. ''I figure we don't have a whole lot to worry about til we start seein' his tracks. When he gets ready to spring his trap, he'll lay us a trail right through the door.''

That's my trouble. Always figurin'. The only trouble was, the Other One was figurin', too.

It was the middle of the afternoon on the third day when we missed O'Leary. He was there, then he was gone. When you ride enough miles with a man, you get to where you feel him beside you as much as seein' him or anything. All of a sudden I had an empty feelin'. I didn't have to look long to see that the Llano had swallowed up O'Leary, horse and all.

I yelled for Dominguez and went for a look. Sure enough, an arroyo split the earth where O'Leary should have been. From forty feet away, the arroyo was completely invisible, but the gully was ten feet wide and deep enough to hide horse and rider. The bottom was as flat as the sides were steep. It was like the silt in the bottom of a giant mud puddle had shriveled and cracked. Maybe it had.

There were horse tracks on the bottom of the arroyo, but no visible way down. I started backtracking along the rim. Dominguez caught up with me in time to discover O'Leary's body. I was still searchin' the arroyo bottom and had just spotted where the horse made his way down when I heard Dominguez holler.

"Madre de Dios!"

He looked like he was asleep. Even his mouth was turned up in a little smile, like he might have been enjoying a pleasant dream. There wasn't even much blood on the back of his shirt, around the wound. The knife had slid between the ribs to the heart and out again. There were only the tracks in the sandy soil to tell the story of the struggle. We could see where the Other One lay hidden until O'Leary rode by, then sprang to the back of the saddle. By the time he was seated, O'Leary was dead. By the time the body hit the ground, the Other One was riding the horse into the arroyo. He chose his place well. It might be miles

97

in either direction before there was another place where a horse could be ridden to the narrow bottom of the ditch.

There it was. Put to us. The tracks were temptations to do Satan himself proud. They lured us as sure as Eve tempted Adam. I've known men who taked to horses like they expected to get an answer, but I had never known anyone to talk to tracks in the dirt. But like a fool, there I sat, talkin' to those tracks and not likin' the answers I was gettin'.

"No sir," says I, "You'd like that wouldn't you? Leadin' me to a trap where you could circle back and jump me from above. Well, I ain't buyin'. Sooner or later, you're gonna come out of that ditch. I'll just foller along on top and catch where you come out."

Dominguez looked at me kind of funny, or like he was thinkin' *I* was kinda funny. "But Señor Laliker, he is just a few moments gone. If we ride fast, we can catch him. No?"

"Sure," I said, "and maybe he will catch us. It might be miles before he finds a place to get out of there, and it might be just around the next bend. Whichever, you can count on him backtrackin' and settin' a trap when he does get out."

"But if one of us rides on the bottom and one on the top, we can cover each other."

I had some ideas of my own about Dominguez' plan workin', but I kept them to myself. Ideas like, what if the arroyo split and the rider on top couldn't follow? And, what if the way up led to the opposite side of the arroyo and the rider on top was completely cut off? And, what good did it do O'Leary to be ridin' on the level when the Indian jumped him?

"What about O'Leary?" I asked.

"He will wait. He has no reason to hurry anymore. If we catch the Indian, we will come back and bury

Señor O'Leary. If the Indian catches us, he will forgive us for not returning.''

"But the buzzards—?''

"They are cowardly creatures. They will watch for days for any movement before they dare come close. And the coyote will not come until the stink drives away the man smell.''

He could tell I wasn't convinced, so he added. "Besides, what is the difference, to be eaten by the buzzards on top of the ground, or by the worms under the ground?''

That didn't do a whole lot to ease my mind, but it was a thing I couldn't argue with. And time was gettin' shorter and the distance between us the the Other One was gettin' longer. The time was botherin' me more than the distance. I knew for a fact, somewhere up ahead, the Indian would wait for us. I just didn't know where. And I didn't want to give him time enough to lay any better trap than I had to.

It took spurs and the lash of the reins to drive my horse over the rim of the arroyo. Even the comparatively easy slope there was so steep, I was forced to lean so far back in the saddle, it seemed like my back was about flat on the horse's rump. Of course it wasn't, but I knew I was committed. A horse might be forced up a climb like that, but he could never make it with a rider on his back.

I spurred my horse to a ground-eating trot. Sure it was hard to keep from layin' on the whip in an all-out push to catch the Other One before he could get out of the ditch or set a trap. But everywhere there was a bend in the arroyo, it looked like I was ridin' head first into a solid dirt wall. Then at the last minute, the wall would yield, sendin' the arroyo and the tracks I followed off in a new direction.

For four or five miles, I rode with nothin' for company except the dirt walls of the arroyo. Then, as suddenly as it began, the arroyo ended. O'Leary's frightened horse stood wild-eyed and panicky, trapped against the end of the trench. There was no sign of the Other One and no sounds from above of Dominguez or even his horse. It was about that time, I realized that I had been so wrapped up in my thinkin' that I hadn't listened for Dominguez since I entered the ditch. A lot of cover I had been for him. But it always did seem like things never got really messed up 'til I went to thinkin'.

"Dominguez!" I yelled the name a dozen times without answer and I knew we were in trouble. Like a fool, I had allowed the enemy to separate us. And like the warrior he was, the Other One had taken advantage of my mistake. Somewhere, the Indian had managed to escape the arroyo and left me chasing an empty saddle while he went after Dominguez.

I was gut sick with the knowledge that I could do nothing for the man who had been loyal to me across a thousand miles of half-charted trail, a friend who had suffered with me through the hell of the Mexican prison in Santa Fe and who had not hesitated for an instant in following me in search of a girl he had never even seen, into a land from which few returned.

Two of the best men I had ever hoped to call friends rode with me onto the Llano. Now O'Leary lay dead, and any betting man would give long odds that Dominguez had shared his fate. I had never felt so helplessly trapped in my life. For all I knew, Dominguez was dead and the Other One was sneakin' up on me. And me stuck in that ditch like the ox Preacher talked so much about. Only there wasn't anybody likely to come along and pull me out. Sure, I could climb out easy enough like the Indian had, but I had a problem he didn't have. He knew he wouldn't need his horse anymore. He would either kill Dominguez and take his horse or get killed tryin'. Either way, he wouldn't need the horse, but I would. The last thing I wanted was to be afoot on the Llano Estacado.

As much as I hated it, there was nothing left for me but to backtrack to where I had entered the arroyo. It was the closest thing to a way out I had seen and I wasn't about to be any help to Dominguez stuck in that ditch. Not wantin' to abandon O'Leary's horse, I wished for the rawhide reata Dominguez carried on his saddle, but wishin' didn't help much. I didn't know how I would stop O'Leary's horse when we got to the other end, but I figured to worry about that later. I drove the loose horse up the arroyo at a dead run, figurin' to make up time and make it harder for the Indian to spring his trap if he was waitin' for me somewhere along the way.

I reckon O'Leary's pony wasn't likin' that ditch any more than I was, 'cause as soon as he got to the break where we came down, he went up. Bein' a fair stock horse, my own pony went after the loose horse on the dead run. But that slope was way too steep for a horse and rider, so I quit the saddle, figurin' chasin' a loose horse to be better than layin' under a dead one.

'Course, I wasn't a-fixin' to let those horses get any farther away than I could help, so I did my best to run up the slope after them. My best wasn't much, but I did make it to the top in time for the party.

There was the Indian I called the Other One a-tryin' to grab first one horse then the other, with all hell breakin' loose all around him. It seemed Dominguez had found himself some friends, 'cause there was rifles firin' from three or four different positions at the Indian. That is, they were firin' in his direction, but I knew Dominguez. If he was aimin' on killin' you

101

could bet the Indian would be a long time dead by then. The same went for the other riflemen.

I didn't have any idea who they were, but in that land, at that time, a man's rifle was a part of him. To head out onto the Llano without bein' able to shoot as quick and straight as you could raise your arm and point your finger was the same as goin' out with dyin' on your mind. It wasn't just a matter of keepin' your scalp. It was as simple a thing as eatin'. A man that couldn't bring down his own game couldn't figure on eatin' too steady.

There were plenty of pronghorns and mule-eared deer, but a man had to shoot straight and fast and far if he figured on venison. There wasn't much trick to gettin' close enough to a buffalo for an easy shot, but they took a whole lot of killin. And there ain't much way a guy can get any deader than havin' a ton of wounded buffalo stompin' around on his back.

Anyway, there he was. The Indian who had taken the Baxter girl was twenty feet away with an empty gun and no more weapon than his skinnin' knife. Now, I never killed a man in my life except I figured it was a matter of him dyin' or me. But like the Preacher was fond of sayin', I was "sorely tempted." I can't recall any chore I've ever done that was any harder than lettin' the hammer down on my Patterson Colt.

Now before you go to gettin' ideas that I was some sort of good Samaritan, you've got to remember Annie Baxter. She was somewhere out there in the middle of that two hundred thousand square miles of hell and there wasn't but one man that had any notion where. I didn't figure on the Other One leadin' us to her. Not in a million years. But there's one thing certain about an Indian. It's for certain sure, you never can tell about one. Though chances were a thousand to one against him leadin' us to the girl, there was still the one chance

102

that he might. And as long as there was any chance, I was goin' to do my best to keep from killin' that chance.

I didn't figure the Indian to understand English, but you don't have to be much of a gambler to know when the deck is stacked against you. By my thinkin', with three rifles keepin' him pinned down, he would be quick enough to give up the fight. I figured to just let him know I was behind him and let him take his own time decidin' to throw it in.

"Hey, Indian. Give it up," I yelled.

Figure the look on the face of a kid at the candy counter, knowin' he gets his choice from all he sees. Or picture a drunk with a ten dollar bill and a bar full of whisky to choose from. No . . .The look on the Other One's face was more like the groom a standin' at the altar waitin' for his bridle and her bein' the prettiest sight you ever laid eyes on and a-comin' down that isle just for him.

I'm tellin' you, that Indian was glad to see me. In that second, all the world fell away and there wasn't anybody or anything that mattered but the Indian and me. And life and death. I guess I blinked my eyes 'cause I never saw him snatch the knife from his belt. He was comin' after me like a hog comin' to slop. And my old Colt weighed a ton and a half. My arm didn't want to do nothin' but hang there and me all the while doin' my best to get it raised enough for a shot.

It was like I was standin' off to the side watchin' the whole thing. The Indian was half way there by the time my gun barrel started to tilt upward. My thumb found the hammer and at last it was aimed, but by that time the distance was gone and the Indian's knife was above me making the downward plunge that would send the shining blade to the hilt in my chest. My finger was squeezin' the trigger as I swung the revolver upward in an effort to block the knife. But I was too late. I was a dead man and I knew it. In the same instant I brought the gun up, I tried to jerk my body away from the charging devil, but thre was no way. The rush of his charge carried him over me and even fallin' backward was not enough to allow me to escape.

It was like everything around me was suddenly gone. Even the Indian. In my whole world, there was nothing left but the fist that held the knife, and the knife comin' down and me frozen in my tracks.

And then, out of the long-forgotten past of a split second before, came the roaring boom of my own pistol. The shot snatched the knife from the Indian's hand and slung it away. The force of the man's charge carried his body over mine and we went down in a heap. The Other One landed on top, but rolled right over me, holdin' the wounded hand in his other. It looked like all the fight was gone out of him, but I had already learned my lesson. Before he could get his feet under him, I put him to sleep with a well-placed pistol barrel on the back of his head.

12

Free

Annie Baxter watched the Comanche ride away. His
departure was a strange, almost sad, sequence of
events. From where they were camped on the white
caliche rock cliffs overlooking the lake formed by the
springs of the Portales, he first rode west. Half a mile
from the camp, he staked the horse Annie had ridden
onto the Llano. Then he rode back through the camp
and some distance to the East. Hesitantly, like sorrow
or fear might make him change his mind, he laid his
rifle on the plains. He rode back to the camp and took
the infant from Annie's arms. It was the first time he
had touched the baby since he first thrust it at her so
many days before.

He held the child at arm's length and faced east,
like he might be offering his son to some pagan diety.
If he expected the god to miraculously take the child
up into the heavens, he was disappointed. But surely
he knew the gods would accept only a perfect sacrifice,
and the child he offered was lame. He would face
Laliker without the protection of the gods.

He handed the child ever so gently to the girl. In
all the days he had held the girl captive, his com-
munications were limited to pointing and grunts. Annie
was startled at the sound of the words.

"You take." Pointing first at the rifle, then at the horse, he commanded, "You go."

Watching the Indian ride away, Annie was filled with fear and joy and relief and desperation. She was free. But how would she survive? For the first time in her life, her very survival hung in the balance of the decisions she would make. There was no father or brother, or even captor, to tell her what to do. There was an empty, frightening, nothing inside her. Nor could she explain the burning hunger within her that drove her to follow after the Indian. It was almost a willingness to trade her new freedom for the protection of the man she had come to hate a little less with each passing day. Almost, she was willing, but not quite.

She shook the feeling off and took stock of her situation. She had the goat to provide milk for the child. But her own food supply was less than adequate. Standing Bear killed a young antelope before they reached the springs, but the meat was almost gone. There was not nearly enough to take her back to civilization.

But starvation was a worry for tomorrow, or the next day. Her first concern was the horse. Without the horse she stood no chance. She threw dried grass and buffalo chips on the remnants of the morning fire and let the breeze bring it back to life. With the infant in her arms, she went after the horse. Not for an in instant did she consider leaving the child alone, even for long enough to go after the horse. For, with the departure of the Indian, the child was totally and completely hers.

The urgency of past days was gone from the girl. The fear of her captor that kept her from ever relaxing completely, left with the departure of the Indian. When she had retrieved the horse and the rifle, she knew she should go. To linger was foolish, yet she stayed. How long since her body had felt the soothing of so simple a luxury as a bath?

She washed her clothes and spread them on the rocks to dry. Then she slipped into the water and absorbed the relaxing flow of pure pleasure that no money can buy.

Noon came and went and the shadows pointed their fingers eastward. Toward home. Almost reluctantly, Annie gathered her possessions. They were few, but each was precious. There were the remnants of her petticoat that were essential for the feeding and care of the baby. Then there was the canteen that had hung from her brother's saddle that day so long ago. Only when something like the canteen made her think of his dead body lying beside the road did the hatred come again to her. She hated the savagery in the Indian that had cost her brother his life, but she could not hate the tenderness that came into his eyes in the unguarded moments when he looked upon the child.

Annie had no ready way to carry what was left of the antelope, but not knowing if or when she would again find food, she determined to take it with her. She tore her dress off at the knees and wrapped the meat in the cloth. She soaked the bundle in the flowing spring to cool it as much as she could before she was ready to go. With a determined set to her jaw and an almost masculine force in her stride, she began her impossible trek.

Standing Bear's rifle was a cumbersome sixty-caliber percussion cap weapon. The powder horn was filled and there were plenty of caps, but there were only five balls for the weapon. Five shots wouldn't stand off an enemy siege, but they might provide food. If she could even shoot the gun. It was nothing like the slim small-bore rifle she had cut her teeth on. The weight of the weapon was a terrible thing. Though it

107

might have comforted some long-ago hunter or trapper to heft the young cannon, Annie knew she could never hold it to fire the weapon from her shoulder. If the time came when she needed the gun, she hoped there would also be a rock to rest it on, or a tree limb. But there were no trees on the Llano Estacado, and precious few rocks.

Leading the goat, with her meager supply of possessions tied to her saddle and the baby in her arms, Annie started home. The shadows pointed eastward. As the day passed, even the shadows seemed to become anxious for the girl. They stretched longer and longer as if saying, "Hurry. Hurry. This way. Don't wait." Then like false friends, they abandoned her when the night came and left her to face whatever was ahead all alone.

The evening was warm enough to be comfortable without a fire. But out of ages gone past, mankind carries an instinct that calls for a fire to comfort him when the sun is gone to gaze into and know that here he is separated from the beasts. For man alone can make a fire or put one out. The wild beast can only feel the heat of the fire and fear it. But to build a fire took tools. Flint and steel to strike a spark, or a bow to spin a stick 'til friction ignited a bit of tinder. And Annie had neither flint nor bow nor tinder. Nor fire.

She took the meat from its wrapper and savored it. She had given no thought to the need for fire before she left the springs. But now she was grateful for whatever foresight had caused her to cook the meat on the fire left by the Indian. She feared she would come to the point where she would be glad to sink her teeth into raw flesh. But not yet. She ate sparingly of her provisions and wrapped the remainder for another day.

Feeding and cleaning the baby took only a short

time. When her few chores were done, exhaustion overtook Annie and she slept. Morning brought with it a new intensity to her problems. Her water was nearly gone and she was days from the closest spring she knew of. Even at that, she wasn't sure she could again find the tiny spring in the breaks of the caprock where they had been surprised by the intruder. Fear of dying of thirst almost sent her back to the flowing spring beside the lake. The spring had been good to her. It gave her the sweet cool water that quenched her thirst and soothed her body. Surely she could go back and wait for some one to come for her. But she knew the futility of her desire. For all she knew, no white man even knew of the lake on the Llano. Her only hope was to keep going east and hope for water. Even the stagnant water that hid in the bottoms of a few of the many wet-weather lakes would keep her and her charges alive.

The breeze started around noon. At first it felt good as it carried the heat from Annie's tortured body. By midafternoon the air was full of dust and the breeze had turned into a strong wind. There was no shelter from the ever-stronger push of the wind. The dust in the air became sand and the sand cut into the exposed flesh of her face and hands and legs. It felt like her skin was being stripped from her body. To gain what little protection her clothes could give from the cutting sand, she allowed the horse to turn to the northeast, away from the wind.

The sun was gone as though blown away by the wind. On and on she rode, for there was no place to stop. She had long since given control of her destiny to the horse she rode. She neither guided nor goaded the animal. She rode with eyes closed against the force of the blinding sand. The tiny body cradled in her arms was so still she feared the baby had choked on the dust, but she dared not remove the coverings to see. All she could do was to clutch the tiny infant closer to her own breast, and pray.

Hours into the night, the horse faltered and stumbled, its cargo scattered before the wind. The fall tore the child from Annie's arms. Screaming, "Baby! Baby!" the girl searched the area on hands and knees. Somewhere in the darkness and the flying sand was the baby, so helpless it had not so much as a name. Desperately the girl searched for the child fate had given to her, then so cruelly snatched from her arms. At last the screams of the Indian baby penetrated the roar of the wind and guided the girl to it.

Annie curled her own body around the infant where it lay. There was nothing she could do except to try to protect the child from the cutting sand. Somehow the time passed and took with it the wind and the sand. They slept.

The light of the sun woke Annie. The joy of being alive and finding the baby alive was short. Only a few yards away, her horse stood with its head to the ground and the right foreleg swollen to nearly double size. That the leg was broken was obvious at a glance. The rifle was still tied to the saddle horn. Annie set her teeth and went to the animal. She stripped the saddle off, but her other possessions, including her food, had been lost during the night. She was crying like a baby as she raised the gun to the horse's head.

Not since early the previous morning had Annie eaten. Hunger gnawed at her, but there was nothing to eat. Annie feared starvation even more than she had feared the Indian. The thought of eating raw meat still repulsed her, but she knew she must eat or die. Even horse meat. But even in this, her efforts were frustrated. Standing Bear had left her with a horse and gun, but no knife. In spite of all her efforts, she couldn't cut through the skin of the animal with the sharpest stone she could find. Half a ton of meat lay before her and she was starving to death. In despair, she turned to the goat. But the goat was gone.

The desperation of her plight overwhelmed Annie. But there was still a little water left in the canteen. And, as if to prolong her agony, the canteen was one of the few possessions left to her. Annie squeezed some water into the mouth of the baby, but it did not satisfy the infant's hunger. She drank what was left of the water, then taking only the baby and the empty canteen, she began the long walk home.

The heat of the day soared as Annie staggered eastward. She never knew when the baby she carried stopped crying. It took her whole mental and physical effort to hang onto the bundle and keep stepping. Over and over she fell, each time protecting the child she carried at the cost of gashed arms and legs and face. Each time she got up more slowly than the time before, until the time came when she could not get up again. It was over. All she could do was wait.

Annie heard the horses come, and through sun-struck eyes, she saw the hazy figures surrounding her. She felt the hands as they unclasped her fingers and removed the baby from her arms. She felt cool water on her lips, and the trickle into her mouth. She tried to swallow, but her parched throat was too swollen and she could only gag and cough. Again the water came to her mouth and she let it stay there until it found its own way into her throat.

13

Laliker and the Preacher

The Indian dropped at my feet like a slaughtered ox. I stood over him looking into his face and wonderin' how many times I had seen him before. "Never, really," I told myself. I must have seen him in the battle for the rim of the caprock, and again I got a glimpse of him when he came into my camp after me on my first trip onto the Llanco.

Yet I knew him. No, not his face or his name. I knew the skill of the man who could come into the camp of such skilled plainsmen as Ramirez, Sainz, and Estavan and move about undetected. I knew the courage of the man who feared death only if it took him before he could take me. I knew the determination of the man who followed his prey days and weeks and years if necessary.

And I knew I would have to kill him. My enemy lay at my feet, but I felt no joy. I had no hatred for him. I had no lust for his death. But I knew him. I knew that whatever it was that made him seek me out on my first venture onto the Llano was still there. Somehow, accordin' to the man Ramirez, who had guided me across the Llano and who knew more about the Plains Indians than any other man I had met, I had become the symbol of failure and bad luck to the

112

Comanche. I was "Bad medicine." As long as I lived, the medicine of the Comanche would be weak. To their way of thinkin', the survival of their people depended on my death.

I couldn't see much way of convincin' the Indian of the error in their logic. When I tried to look at it from their viewpoint, I didn't much blame them. Time and again I had faced almost certain death at the hands of the Comanche, yet I lived and many of his brothers lay in their graves. I didn't know whether or not he could speak English, but it didn't seem to matter. What words would make him believe me if I told him I wanted only friendship with the Indians? What difference did it make that I had no magic power over his people? As long as they believed I held the power, no misfortune would be accidental. Any evil or bad luck that befell them would be purely and simply the evil medicine of Laliker.

"Is he dead?"

The question came from my right.

"Preacher," I said, looking around. "It's good to see you. No, I knocked him out."

I could have asked a thousand questions about how he came to be there and about how he had cornered the Indian. But there was no need. I knew the answers. He was there because he was alive, and only death could have kept him from goin' after the girl. And that's the kind of thing men don't talk about. When you have a thing to do, you just do it. The Preacher and me, we rode the river together. We knew each other likefew men ever know even their own brothers. We looked each other in the eye and I knew he was as glad to see me alive and well as I was him.

"Estavan," I said, reaching for the hand of the big black man. "I see you're still takin' care of this overgrown sin-stomper."

113

"Well, I reckon we sort of take care of each other."

If any takin' care of was needed, that was the pair to do it. Either of the giants would cut a swathe through normal men like a scythe through wheat. I figured a grizzly bear would have about as much chance against the two of them as fried chicken at an all-day Baptist meetin'. I mean, they would take him apart and enjoy doin' it.

"Have you seen any sign of the girl?" I asked.

"We were figurin' on askin' you the same question," Preacher answered. "We picked up the Indian's tracks about two miles south of here. They made a big circle and came in here from the east. We found O'Leary's body and your tracks. But we were lucky enough to see the Indian double back and set his trap for you. Dominguez figured it out and came back on the run. He beat us here and started the party. We made ourselves to home and joined in. It looked like everyone was comin' but you. Looks like you got the last dance anyway."

The Indian was stirrin'. Dominguez and Estavan took him aside to tie him and tend to his wounded hand while Preacher and I talked.

"The tracks were plain enough where we cut them, but they may not last. This wind is sure pickin' up. If it gets any worse, we won't have tracks left to follow."

I hadn't even noticed the wind. It had been pushin' on me all the time we talked, but I was so lost in the conversation, I had been unaware of it. Even then it seemed to be gettin' stronger. Dust was kickin' up all around and it was hard to keep my eyes open.

"The closer we are to the girl when we lose the tracks, the less area we will have to search," I said. "Let's head out."

I started for my horse before I noticed the stranger.

No, he wasn't a stranger. It was the young man I had shot against at the fourth of July celebration, Joe Baxter. Annie's brother. "Baxter," I said, extending my hand to him. "The word I had was that you was dead. Glad to see they were wrong."

He took the hand I offered. "Got a bad bump and a headache, was all. I figure to live long enough to put a bullet in the Indian that took Annie."

"Well, I said, "I expect you've noticed by now this particular Indian takes a lot of killin'. Anyway, we've got him now. He won't give us much trouble. And we'll see about puttin' a bullet in him if and when the time comes."

The look in the eyes of the youth was all the testimony I needed to convince me he believed what he said. "I count myself a fair man. I *think* this is the Indian that took my sister. But I ain't sure. The minute I get enough proof to satisfy my own mind, I aim to put a bullet through his head."

"You mean it don't matter to you why he might have taken your sister?"

"Not a bit. If he laid hands on a Baxter woman, he will die for it. The same as you would."

I could see I wasn't too popular with Baxter. It might have been he blamed me for the situation his sister was in. Come to think of it, he was right. If I hadn't led the Other One to her, she would still be safe and free in her own home.

The urgency of the situation broke through our talk. I caught my horse and the others did the same. Baxter didn't seem any more anxious to be close to me than I was to be close to him. I rode at the head of the line and Baxter at the rear.

We made the circle and were headin' west when the wind erased the last traces of the Indian's tracks. The dust in the air had turned to sand. And our hopes of finding the girl, Annie, were being cut away by the driven sand. We were all thinking nearly the same thoughts, though none dared put them into words.

It seemed hopeless. If Annie had been left tied, with no way to find shelter, there was no way she could survive the storm. The windblown sand would cut into any exposed skin and literally strip the flesh from her bones. If she was not tied, she might wander through the storm and become so lost there would be no chance of ever finding her.

We pushed on westward until at last Estavan called a halt. "It's foolish to go on. For all we know, we've passed the spot where the Indian left her. If we go on, we will surely pass her by."

I had been thinkin' similar thoughts, but hadn't dared be the one to stop. "I agree," I said. "We'll camp here with wht shelter we can make, then start our search in the morning."

Nobody had forgotten the Other One. But nobody had been foolish enough to attempt to make him lead us to the girl. We simply tied him to a saddle and took him along. I don't think anyone gave any thought to why we kept him, except what else was there to do? I had no desire to kill him and the others felt the same way. Sure, he took the girl and killed O'Leary and was an all-around bad man. But there was reason to his killing. If he was a renegade that killed for the sake of killing, we would have felt no regrets at ridding the country of him. At least not too many regrets. But to him, we were involved in war. A war for the survival of his people that was just as real to him as if we had regiments of troops lined up facin' each other.

Except maybe Joe Baxter. I reckon Joe would have shot him down, except he wasn't sure we had the right Indian. I was.

But we couldn't have him runnin' loose on the plains

to cause us more trouble, so about all we could do was to keep him prisoner. It worked out for the best, though. Just as we were decidin' to make camp, we got a surprise that nearly knocked us right out of our saddles.

The Indian spoke. "The white woman is at the water beside the white rocks."

I knew the place. We camped there on the way to Sante Fe a year before. But I couldn't find it again without landmarks. Expecially in the midst of the worst sand storm I had ever seen. "Will you take us there?" It seemed strange for the Indian to suddenly break his silence and speak to us in English. But somehow it didn't seem strange for me to question him in the same language. Or, for that matter, even to be talking to one who had tried to kill me such a short time before. In answer, he held his wrists out to me in an obvious request to have his bonds cut. I responded as automatically as when I asked him to lead us. My knife slashed through the leather thongs in a quick and easy stroke.

"Did you leave the woman tied?"

"No. White woman has horse and gun of Standing Bear. She has papoose of Standing Bear. She is good woman. Strong. Will not die in sand. But maybe papoose will die. There is shelter, but woman can not find. We go to her."

I don't know if Baxter was close enough to hear what the Indian said or not. Anyway, he made no attempt to carry through on his promise to kill the Indian the minute he had proof of his guilt. It could be he had the presence of mind to realize our need of the Comanche, at least until we found the girl.

"What makes you think she stayed at the lake?"

"From long way off I look back. Woman not leave

117

lake. She wait for Standing Bear to come back. She my woman.''

I couldn't help it. I felt the hackles rise on the back of my neck. I was closer to killin' him right then than I had ever been before. It was nothin' but pure jealousy, and I knew it. But knowin' it didn't help much and it took me a little while to get control of myself. After all, I had only seen the girl one time. Who was I think of her as my woman? But I did.

I turned my horse aside and let the Indian take the lead. At last I had a name for him. Standing Bear. He seemed a little less awesome with a name. Though Standing Bear was a fine name, representing bravery and strength and pride, it didn't conjure up the visions if invincibility of the Other One. With a real name, he was just a man.

I rode beside the Indian who hated me. But for a little while we each had the same enemy—the wind. The driving, howling wind, pushing us back and laughing at us all the way, trying to turn us back at every step. And the sand that cut and tore at our eyes and choked off our breath and beat against us like millions of tiny cannon balls bouncing against a mountain until at last the mountain must crumble before them. With each step we had to force the horses onward. The sand was blinding them and they didn't have our reasons for pushing on. Only whip and lash and spur kept them going. But it wasn't long before the pain and fear of the storm was greater than what we could, or were willing to, do to them. They quit.

On foot, leading the blindfolded horses, we pushed on, but it seemed hopeless. I think I would have given up a thousand times over, except for the constant presence of the others. I looked from man to man and saw no sign of quitting in any of them.How could I do less? Without complaint, I stumbled on.

118

Ahead of me, Standing Bear fought the wind. To him it was an old enemy, many times fought and many times defeated. He leaned into the force of it with a confidence that made me wonder at such a thing as pitiful man challenging the wrath of nature. But hour after hour, mile after mile, he led on. Somewhere in the dark I lost the hours and the miles and all that was important was the one step I had to take to keep from falling, and the one breath I had to draw to stay alive.

And then we were there. Spread before us was the lake of the Portales. Directly beneath us were the low white cliffs from which the springs flowed to fill the lake. But there was no sign of Annie. We searched the shore line, but had no luck. At last even Standing Bear gave up. At the base of the white cliff, at the very edge of the water, we huddled together beneath a makeshift tent made from our ground tarps. Surely the coming of a new day would signal the end of the storm.

14

More Indian Troubles

When morning came the wind was gone, the sand was gone—and the Indian was gone.

Sure, I tied him. And I would have sworn no man could escape from my knots. But like most things you swear by, I found myself eatin' my own words.

It was a thing to ponder, though. Standing Bear could have taken anything he wanted, including our horses and our lives. Yet no weapon was missing except his own knife, and the rifle he had taken when he killed O'Leary. And no horse was gone save the mount of O'Leary. To the victor goes the spoils and evidently Standing Bear considered the possessions of O'Leary to be his now.

We spent the day searching the area for signs of Annie Baxter. Our horses were so used up that we didn't dare follow Standing Bear the first morning. To an Indian, a horse was a thing to be used until it was used up, then to be eaten or discarded, whichever was the handiest. But we had no intention of searching the whole Llano on foot or walking all the way back to the wagon we left below the cap. So we rested the horses. A day on that rich grama grass with all the water they wanted would erase most of the effects of the storm.

Our search yielded just what we expected, hoped for, and feared. Nothing. If Annie was ever anywhere near the lake, the wind had completely erased all signs of her stay. No track, no bit of cloth, no hidden messages. Nothing said she had ever been near except the word of Standing Bear. It was enough. We believed the Indian when he told us of leaving the girl at the lake, and we had no reason to change our minds.

The tracks we followed away from the spring-fed lake led us north and east.

Estavan interpreted the Indian's reasoning for choosing the direction he took. "If the girl rode out of here on a horse, she would have to give her horse its head. The storm would drive them with it. No one could force a horse to head any other direction in such a wind."

But how far had she gone before the storm struck? If she headed east in an attempt to return home, she might have been a day's ride or more away before the storm turned her toward the North.

"I figure if she's alive, Standing Bear will find her," I told them. "It seems to me the best thing to do would be to follow the Indian."

"He'll find her all right," Estavan said. "The only question is, will she be dead or alive?"

"What do you think, Estavan?" Preacher asked. "Have you got some other idea?"

"The girl probably rode east out of here. That's easy enough to figure. And the storm most likely turned her north. That is, unless she found some shelter. And shelter ain't easy to come by out here."

"Sure," I said. "But we still don't know how far east she went before she turned north."

"If we ride behind the Indian half a day and find no sign of the woman, one of us should head east. Then another one should go east at the middle of the

121

afternoon. And another when the sun comes up to-morrow. One man is enough to follow the Indian. If the girl is alive she will make tracks on the plains. If there are tracks we will find them.''

He didn't add that if she was hurt and layin' out there somewhere she wouldn't make tracks. He didn't need to. We all knew the impossibility of finding her if she left no trail. She would die on the Llano and no man would ever find even her bones.

Dominguez was the first to turn east. One thing we didn't want was men scattered all over the plains and nobody knowin' who went where. It was agreed that each man would hold a straight line east. If he cut the tracks of the girl, he would follow them. If not, he would go on to the caprock where Sam, the cook, waited with his wagon. We told Dominguez to head back to the settlements if we didn't get to the wagon within three days of him. Of course we knew neither Sam nor Dominguez would head back as long as there was any chance they might be needed. Anyway, the whole idea was to keep them from coming out after us if we didn't make it back.

Estavan was persuaded to be next to turn away from the tracks we followed. He didn't like it much, but since it was his plan he couldn't very well refuse to folow it. He had the same instructions about headin' back to the settlements, but it wasn't hard to see in his eyes that he wouldn't be likely to leave without us. Without Preacher, anyway.

Two hours later, Joe Baxter turned east. His hatred for the confessed kidnapper of his sister drove him after the tracks. Only the hope of finding his sister alive compared to the uselessness of revenge made him turn away. I could have told him about the value of keeping Standing Bear alive to help us search if we didn't find Annie, but I knew the futility of it. No argument would convince him the world might be a better place with the Comanche alive, not even for a little while. From the first light he cursed himself for not killing the Indian while he had the chance. To hint at trying to capture Standing Bear alive was not the argument to use to convince Baxter to head east.

It was good to ride beside Preacher. He had a strength about him that was more than a reflection of his size and the power of his body. It was a thing that seemed to radiate from him like the heat from a camp fire. You might call it evidence of his confidence in his own abilities, or you might say it was a reflection of his faith in the God he served. Whatever you called it, you couldn't deny it. Preacher was a man with something about him.

We finished the day without incident. Prairie dogs and owls, with an occasional coyote or hawk, were the only signs of life on the Llano. And the tracks.

Standing Bear's horse faltered in late afternoon. The tracks told their story of an animal pushed beyond its limit. Each mile we expected to come upon the body of the animal. Yet he went on. We wondered, but we didn't talk about what cruel torture Standing Bear must have used on the horse to drive him so far past what a horse could normally endure.

Just before the sky dropped out from under the sun, we found the carcass. Even in death, the animal had served Standing Bear. Half of one hindquarter had been cut away. The ashes told of the feast the Indian enjoyed at the expense of his mount. The moccasin tracks leading from the camp pointed due east. The Bear had turned.

We followed the moccasin tracks in the morning light. It was a slow process. The tracks were only a hint of the passage of the man. If Standing Bear had chosen to do so, he could easily have made it impossible for us to follow. But either he didn't care or he was deliberately layin' trail for us. It did seem as though he would have stepped on soft sand a little more often, though, if he wanted us to follow.

For two or three hours, we puzzled out the trail. But we were makin' such slow progress, we knew we would never catch the Indian, even with him on foot. My patience broke first.

"What do you think about forgettin' the tracks? Let's just head east in a lope and see if we catch up to him."

"I've been thinkin' the same," Preacher answered. "Only what if he suddenly cuts off in some other direction? Or lays a trap for us?"

"I figure he's got his mind on Annie and the baby. He's made up his mind to have her for his woman. And he was as anxious about his son in that sandstorm as we were about Annie. To my way of thinkin', he's about as worried about them right now as we are."

"What do you think about splittin' up? If one of us was to go on ahead, maybe the other ought to stick with the tracks."

I vetoed that idea real quick. "Not on your life. I figure we're too close to winnin' or losin'. Whatever is to come will be today. We'll either find Annie or we'll find out there ain't no use in lookin' anymore. Either way, I think we can handle it better if we stick together."

He nodded his head, "I figured the same, but I thought it was worth mentionin'. Let's go find that girl."

We spurred our mounts into a lope. It was really more of a fast walk, but we were finally coverin' the ground.

I couldn't help watchin' for Standing Bear's tracks, but at the pace we were makin' there wasn't a chance of seein' any. It was temptin' to slow down and look occasionally. But the decision had been made. We would push on to the rim of the Llano. If we didn't find signs of the girl before we reached the caprock, we knew it would be hopeless. We tried to avoid thinkin' of that.

She was out there someplace and she was alive and alone. And scared. We had to find her. I wouldn't let myself think of any other possibility.

The tracks were anything but what we expected. Instead of the tracks of a lone horse or woman on foot, it looked like an Indian tribe on the move. There were many unshod ponies and a few with shoes. The scratch marks of several travois testified to the presence of women and children with all their possessions. Estavan could have told the difference between the men and the women, but there is little about a moccasin track to to tell of the size or weight of the wearer. I was not that skilled. Neather was Preacher.

We staked our horses away from the trail so we could study the tracks. Even an unskilled eye can learn a lot from tracks if they are studied closely enough.

I had a go once at readin' a little of the law. There were a lot of things in there I could sort out pretty clear, and there were a lot more I couldn't. Things like *torts* and *habeas corpus* and all sorts of words that surely meant something to somebody, but they didn't mean a thing to me. Tryin' to read those tracks wasn't much different.

Sure, it was obvious about it bein' a whole tribe on the move. And the number of horses made it clear they were Plains Indians. Their direction said they were headed after the herds of buffalo which had already gone north. But were they Comanche or Kiowa? Or some other tribe? Estavan could have read it in the tracks. And what about the shod horses? Probably stolen in a raid somewhere far to the south.

But why were they so late in following the buffalo? Maybe they were Standing Bear's tribe and they had waited for him. But if his tribe was so close, why hadn't he left the baby with the squaws? And why didn't he take Annie Baxter to them instead of leaving her alone to care for his child on the Llano? The more I pondered the situation, the more confused I got. Preacher kept a clearer head and a sharper eye.

"What do you make of this?"

His question brought me back to the problem at hand. I looked carefully at the tracks he pointed out. They were small. Too small for a man, but too large for a child. They were made by a woman or a youth.

And they were different. Unlike the shapeless imprint of the Indian moccasin, they were sharp edged and they clearly showed a raised heel. The tracks of a white woman, or at least a white woman's shoes. She was with the Indians. Her tracks were mixed with the tracks of horses and travois and moccasins. If she had been merely following the trail left by the tribe, her tracks would be on top of the others.

Like those of the man.

The moccasin tracks were harder to separate from the confusion of tracks, but they lay on top. No horse track travois mark nor other footprint covered any track laid by the man. And he was in a hurry. The length of his stride and the obvious impact of his foot striking the softened earth testified to the fact that whoever made the tracks was running. Estavan could have looked at the tracks and told if he had ever seen them before. But I didn't need his skill to identify the the tracks.

It was Standing Bear. The Other One. He was somewhere ahead of us and running after the Indians who now held Annie. The urgency of his stride pulled at me. I wanted to spur my horse after him in an effort to run him down and snatch the girl from him and his people. But it was well past noon and our horses were near spent. Sure, they had the rest of the day left in them, and more too. With water and graze and rest, they could go on for many more days. But not if we ran them into the ground in one desperate attempt to overtake Standing Bear.

It was almost too easy. Following the Indians, I mean. The trail was clear and smooth and straight. Though whatever tribe they might be was movin' fast, we were rapidly gaining on them. Late in the day we were surprised to realize the haze ahead of was was not haze at all, but the dust stirred up by the movin' Indians. In less than half an hour, we would overtake them.

That wouldn't do at all. We needed the cover of darkness to slip in close enough to estimate their numbers and to try to locate where Annie Baxter was being held. I reckon I read too much into the shoe prints, but any possibility other than her bein' alive and well was too foreign for me to accept.

While we were stopped to worry out out next move, we noticed Standing Bear was gone. Somewhere back down the line, we had either passed him or he had left the trail. Or maybe he had already caught up with his friends. I sure was wishin' I knew which, but there wasn't much use worryin' about it. I didn't figure it would be easy to get Annie away from the Indians without them knowin' we were comin'. Standing Bear warnin' them about us couldn't make it a whole lot harder.

The day had been long and the night didn't promise to be any shorter. We were hungry and tired and our mounts were nearly done in. It seemed only logical to stop where we were to rest up. We had water and jerked beef, but I questioned the wisdom of makin' a fire when Preacher suggested we make a broth from the jerky. My objections fell apart like smoke in the wind when Preacher produced a package of coffee from somewhere in his pack. I would fight a hundred Comanches for a cup of the black acid Preacher called coffee.

The sun was still a ways above the horizon, but we knew we would need what sleep we could get. You've probably figured out by now that arguin' with Preacher was about the biggest waste of time a feller could get into. Well, I didn't argue much when he insisted I be the first to sleep. What was the use? I figured to pretend I was asleep for a while then act like I woke up feelin' frisky as a week-old colt. I laid down on my blankets and closed my eyes. About two minutes later he was shakin' me and tellin me to get up. I swear I never had time to doze off, but if I didn't, he sure worked somethin' on me. The sun was gone and the stars were blinkin' at me like they don't do anywhere else on earth. I mean, you've never seen the stars till you've laid on your back out in the clear clean air of the Llano and gazed into the night sky. The sun sets out there spread all the way from north to south as far as the eye can see. And the colors make the rainbow look like faded laundry. They would make any man, even Preacher, tongue-tied, just tryin' to describe them. But the sunsets ain't nothin' compared to the stars.

Preacher said, ''Wake me up when the moon comes out.'' He barely made it to his blankets and was asleep by the time his head touched the ground.

I was more rested than I knew a man could get in such a short time. I sure wanted to push on, lookin' for the Indian camp, but there was no way. Preacher had earned his rest and it was mine to stand guard over him. I didn't dare go even to the top of the nearest hill to try to spot the fires of the Indian camp.

I sat beside the cold remains of our fire, huddled in my blanket. The heat had long since left the ashes, but still they held me close. Out in the darkness the air was filled with the contented sound of Preacher's mule and my horse pullin' off the grass and noisily chewin' it.

For the first time in days I was free to let my mind wander. I couldn't help thinkin' about the girl. The picture I thought would never fade from my mind was gone. Did she have freckles? Or dimples? Did her eyes really sparkle like a mountain stream bouncing over the rocks on a bright summer day? And would you call her hair blond or light brown?

It seemed silly that I could answer none of the questions in my mind. I was beginin' to wonder if I would even recognize her when I saw her again. Of course I would. She looked like—What did she look like? What had made me think I loved her? And what made the fires of jealously burn inside me when Standing Bear spoke of her as his woman?

The questions were there but the answers were not. I had long since lost track of time. Days or weeks had become unimportant. Only tomorrow counted. To-morrow, or another tomorrow, I would find Annie and I would free her. What did it matter if I died in the trying? My life had become so simple. I existed for but one purpose. At any cost Annie Baxter would be free.

15

Estavan

A glance told Estavan the tracks were not Comanche. Probably Kiowa, he reasoned. They were the only Indians strong enough to challenge the Comanche for hunting rights on the Llano, except for the Apache. But the Apache never traveled in such numbers. An Apache tribe might number in the hundreds, but they never traveled in bunches of more than a dozen or so. The smaller groups gave them freedom to go where food and water was more scarce. And of all the peoples of earth, freedom was most sacred to the Apache.

Estavan turned his mule into the wake of the Indian tribe. If the Indians, whoever they might be, crossed the path of the girl, they would search her out. If they did not find her, then Estavan knew he could do no better. To search further would be a cruel torture of the dumb mule he rode.

A few miles from where he picked up the trail of the Indians, Estavan found the carcass of Annie's horse. The broken leg and the bullet hole in the animal's head told the story of the troubles the rider had known. The tracks of the girl told who the rider had been.

So Standing Bear had spoken the truth. He had freed the girl and given her a gun. But she was no longer free. Estavan knew she was eather dead or a captive of the Indians. And he held none of Laliker's romantic notions about the probability of her being still alive. Still, he would not turn from the search as long as there was a chance.

More miles to the north he came upon the new tracks. Another rider had crossed the trail left by the migrating tribe. The tracks were deep cut in the sand. They told the story of heroic but foolish effort on the part of the rider. Under spur and whip, the horse ran at full gallop in pursuit of the Indians. That the rider had not the experience to know the tracks were hours old was obvious. The headlong rush of the rider convinced Estavan that it must have been young Baxter.

Besides, Preacher rode a mule and Laliker was a thinking man. Even if he had been foolish enough to run the life out of his horse, Laliker would have stopped to think it over first.

The tracks of the white woman mingled with those of the Indians and their horses. And Estavan knew. The girl was alive and well. Her step was firm and sure. And she moved freely from side to side in the group. If she were being dragged behind a brave's pony, her step would show the stumbling gait of one who struggles to keep standing to prevent being dragged to death. And if her mind was gone, as had happened to the Wilson girl, she would have been driven from among the people long before so many miles were covered.

The epic written in the sands grew sinister with the entry of the Comanche. The moccasin tracks lay over the tracks of the people, but under the tracks of Joe Baxter's horse. Baxter's tracks showed no sign that he had seen those of the Indian. Though his horse was faltering regularly by that time, there was nothing to indicate he ever slowed to investigate the tracks.

131

The horse stood spread-legged with head hanging nearly to the ground. Baxter's saddle, bridle, and bedroll lay in a heap nearby. The only sign of the man was the trail of boot prints pointing the way north after the Indians.

Estavan poured his hand full of water and held it to the horse's muzzle. The soft lips quivered and the water was gone. Few men shared either Estavan's love for animals or his understanding of them. Only those few men could understand the thrill inside the dark-skinned man when the horse took the water. The animal would live.

Another handful, then a hatful. Estavan drove the horse to a spot where the grama was the thickest and left him eating. There was plenty of grass. Water was a problem but within half a day's walk in any direction there were a dozen or more playa lakes. Some had a little water in the bottom. What did it matter to a horse if the water was green and smelled of the manure of the buffalo who used the lakes for refuge from the heat of the sun and the bite of the fly?

If he regained his strength before he was found by a lobo wolf, or by a pack of coyotes, or a panther or cougar, the horse would live. He would live if he stayed away from the rattlesnake and managed to avoid stepping in the hole of a prairie dog or gopher or badger.

Estavan stood beside his mule and pondered the new tracks. The huge boot tracks could only have been made by Preacher, and the lesser ones by Laliker. Estavan read the story of their discovery of the tracks of the girl and those of Standing Bear. He saw the tracks of their mounts laid upon those of the Indian, and the tracks of Joe Baxter over all the others.

When Standing Bear's tracks separated themselves from the maze, neither Laliker nor Preacher noticed.

Only Estavan's sharp eye was quick enough to catch the sudden absence of the almost invisible prints. Estavan wrestled with the problem in his mind. He wasn't long in deciding his only route. If the Baxter girl could be rescued, Laliker and Preacher could do it. But as long as the Indian, Standing Bear, lived, his friend would never be out from under the threat of death. A shudder went through the huge black body. The thought of hunting the Indian down was about as comforting as the idea of taking a nap in a den of rattlers.

But it was a thing to be done. Estavan turned his mule in the direction the tracks led. To be warned is to be armed. And Estavan had fair warning in the skills of his quarry. The man was a master of deceit and camouflage. Hc had the patience of the stream that knows that by and by, little by little, the mountain will yield and go with it to the sea. Nor did Estavan underrate Standing Bear's skill with the knife he carried, the skill that had sent O'Leary to a graveless death on the plains. How many more hardened fighting men had been sent to their death at the hand of Standing Bear was a thing to guess at. It was not Estavan's intention to join them.

He stopped his mule to study the tracks ahead. Then satisfied, he drove the hated, but necessasary spurs home to the ribs of his mount. At other times he cautiously followed the tracks in an attempt to read the signs of potential ambush. Then he would ride far to the right or left of the track, constantly changing his pattern to make it harder for Standing Bear to lay in wait for him.

The pace set by Standing Bear never changed. He was covering the ground in a mile-consuming walk. He was a man with a goal in mind. There was never any indication that he might turn back and wait for pursuit. There was no sign he meant to hide his trail or deliberately make tracking him easy. The tracks he left said he was a man with things on his mind and places to go.

Estavan hungered to forget the caution that dragged at him like an anchor. Everything about the trail he followed told him to push on. Hurry. Somewhere on the plains ahead of him the drama was being acted out. And like a man with a book, he was left to read the story printed in the sand.

Once again the tracks of Standing Bear followed the unknown tribe. And again the tracks of Laliker and Preacher lay upon those of Standing Bear. And the tracks of Joe Baxter covered them all. Baxter could be only a short distance ahead. Afoot he would be falling farther behind.

Estavan spurred his mule to a faster pace. Still he kept cautious eyes searching the plains as far ahead as he could. He was no longer fearful of Indian ambush, with friends between him and the Indian. But to suddenly overtake any armed man in such a tense situation was dangerous. A bullet fired in haste by a friend would kill just as dead as one deliberately fired by an enemy.

Estavan approached the prone figure like a hunter circling a wounded bear. It was easy to see the man was Joe Baxter. What was hard to see was whether or not Baxter was alive. And if he was alive, was he unconscious or faking? Could Baxter tell friend from foe? And really, how well did he know Baxter? Many a man would kill their best friend for less than a mule if it meant a better chance to rescue his sister from Indian captivity.

The black man poured his own hand full of water and let the precious fluid drip onto Baxter's lips.

An hour of careful nursing and doling out water brought young Baxter back into the world. But their problems were a long way from over. They were days from help and had only one mule between them. The animal might have carried two small men, but one thing Estavan wasn't was small. Their only hope for survival seemed to be in heading back to Sam's wagon.

"You take your mule and you go on back," Joe Baxter said. "There ain't no power on this earth can make me leave without my sister."

"I reckon you figure on bein' a lot of help to her, layin' dead on the prairie." The words of the Negro were words of wisdom, but Baxter was beyond reason.

"I ain't scared of your Indian. He got the jump on me once, but I'll be ready for him next time."

"Will you be ready for dyin' of thirst like if I hadn't come along?"

Guilt reddened the youth's face. "I know I owe you. And I'll pay you back if I get the chance. But first I aim to have Annie free."

"You've got your head set on goin' then? There ain't no chance of talkin' you out of it?"

"You know there ain't. As long as there's a chance in a million, I got to try."

"I would be mighty disappointed if you didn't feel that way," Estavan surprised Baxter by saying. "The only two friends I ever had in my life are out there. More than anything else in this world, I want to go help them if they need me. But I owe it to you to take you back to the wagon if you want to go."

"You just head out after Preacher and Laliker and see how fast I come along."

"There ain't no use goin' today. It would be dark before we could get two miles. I figure to lay over close by and get a good start in the mornin'. My mule needs the rest even if you don't."

Estavan led the mule with its burden to the bottom

135

of the playa lake. Sure enough, there was a puddle of green water there.

"Too many antelope around for no water," he answered the question Baxter hadn't gotten around to asking. "It was just a matter of findin' the right hole. All it took was brains and a ton of luck."

Estavan gathered buffalo chips and built a fire. From somewhere in his pack, the trail-wise man produced coffee and a pot. Estavan let the water boil a long time before he threw the handful of coffee grounds into the pot. The brew was thick, but the coffee killed most of the taste. They tried to avoid thinking of what all might be in the water. Like it or not, the green water would keep them alive. Estavan's canteens, emptied in nursing Baxter back to life, were filled with the fluid after it was boiled a long time. The mule stood knee deep in the water and drank his fill. Occasionally he looked up at the men as if he was inviting them to drink with him, but they declined the offer.

In the light of day, they again took the trail. Baxter rode the mule while Estavan trotted alongside, hanging onto the saddle. After an hour the men switched positions. On through the day they went until midafternoon. The distant sound of shots sent them hurrying to the top of a low hill. They could see the dust of a running gun battle out on the plains, but could not tell who the combatants were. The odds were strong in favor of Laliker an Preacher being mixed up in it. The action was coming their way, so they staked the mule and dug in. They hoped they weren't buying into the wrong fight.

16

The Bear is Dead

I left Preacher and circled around the camp. Early in the morning we got a glimpse of Annie Baxter among the Indian women. She seemed free enough in bein' allowed to move around camp, but we figured she would find out just how much of a prisoner she was if she tried to walk away. I reckon she knew that too, 'cause she never tried it. Either that or she had sense enough to know how much better off she was with the Indians than she would be wanderin' around the Llano without water or a horse.

It was a thing to watch. One minute there were twenty tepees standing out there on the plains. Almost in the next, they were gone and the whole tribe was on the move.

Me and Preacher didn't know how we would get Annie away from the Indians. But we did know that things seem to work themselves out if a man is patient enough. So the way we figured it was to bide our time and watch. Whichever one of us saw a way first was to go ahead. Then the other would follow his lead.

A lot of things crossed my mind while I tried to figure a way to get Annie out. I thought about sneakin' in and tryin' to get out without bein' seen. I forgot that silly idea about as quick as I had it. And I thought about gettin' ahead of them and tryin' to hide so when they came by I could grab Annie and run. That idea seemed about as worthless as my tryin' to sneak into the camp.

The only idea that seemed like it might have any chance of workin' was to just ride in among them and try to dicker for Annie's release. But I didn't have a whole lot to dicker with. I decided to try it anyway if no better idea came by the time the Indians made camp for the night. I thought of a thousand things as I followed Annie's captors. About the only thing I didn't think of was the Other One. Standing Bear.

One minute the prairie was empty for miles around me. The next minute he was makin' like his name. He stood twenty feet ahead of me, just darin' me to come any closer. He was standin' all spread-legged in my path with his knife held ready at his side. Sure I could have shot him to pieces before he got close enough to use his knife. But as surely as I killed him, I would kill Annie, because the Indians that held her were movin' up a draw less than a quarter mile away. Even if they didn't kill her immediately, we would never get inside their camp after they heard the shots.

Standing Bear knew me pretty good by then and I figure he knew he had me. It was fight him his way or send Annie to her death.

I carried a belt knife 'cause a man livin' off the land is hard put to do without one. A man's knife wasn't a sissy little thing carried for show. It had to be big enough and have enough weight to hack through firewood or buffalo bone. The steel chosen for the blade had to be hard enough to hold its edge through six weeks of choppin' and hackin' on everything from beef brisket to post oak, and still be sharp enough to slice the belly of a slippery trout when a man got hungry.

If I chose a knife to fight with, I would most likely have chosen the same knife that filled my hand. It was a friend that had stood beside me for most of the years of my life. I knew how to swing it just the right way to fell a young pine in a single blow, and how to delicately slice through the skin of a deer or elk and to twist and turn the handle, guiding the razor-sharp blade, skinnin' the animal out, never cuttin' flesh or skin. With that knife I once sliced a bull hide into a single strip a quarter inch wide and many yards long. The same hide was braided into the reata that hung from Dominguez's saddle and was his pride and joy.

I had done about all that could be done with a knife, except fight. I never wanted no more than my fists in a fight except one time. I mean man-to-man fights, not shootin' fights. I had sure done my share of fightin' with a gun. But the only time I ever wanted more than fists in a hand-to-hand fight was that time Preacher decided to pin my hide to the wall. But a weapon wouldn't have done me any good that time. I was whipped and layin' stone cold on the ground before I could have used a knife anyway.

But there I was, up against it. I would knife-fight Standing Bear, or watch my guts spill out on the ground.

I was a little sad standin' there facin' the Indian. I knew we would struggle and one would win and the other would lose. Blood would flow into the sand and take with it his life or mine. And nothing would be gained. A useless death. Tasks left undone. Preacher left alone to try to rescue Annie. Or the useless death of the Indian at the hand of a man who wanted only to take the girl back to her home. I had no desire to kill him. But kill I would, if it took that to stay alive long enough to rescue Annie.

We circled each other with knives flashin' in the

sun. Standing Bear flashed a broken-toothed grin at me. "The mighty Laliker is not so fearsome without his pistol. The fear shows in your eyes. Why do you not use the pistol?"

Of course he knew the answer to his question. He had laid his trap well and forced me into his kind of fight. The knife in his hand was as quick and deadly as a pistol in mine. I had the instincts of the fighting man, but so had he. So what if he had a slight limp? He was in no foot race. The speed he needed for the battle at hand was the quickness in moving the fraction of an inch that turned death into a miss. I thrust and hacked at him, but he laughed. Every jab he blocked with his blade, every chopping hack missed by the width of a hair as his body weaved forward and backward and from one side to the other.

The sun was high and it burned without mercy on our flesh. Sweat ran down my face and into my eyes. But I dared not even wipe a sleeve across my forehead to cut off the flow. To blind myself for a split second would be to see my bones left to bleach in the sun.

Sweat made the knife handle slippery in my aching hand. The wetter it got the more slippery it got, and the tighter I had to grip it to keep the weapon from flying away. And the tighter I gripped the more my forearm and shoulder ached from the effort.

Time and again we locked in combat. His iron grip held my knife hand useless, but neither was he able to get his knife hand free from my own left hand that grasped his wrist. Each time my greater size and strength won out, but before I could drive my blade home, he managed to step just beyond the reach of my knife.

For Standing Bear, the fight was the end of a year of hate and waitin' and sufferin'. It was what he had lived for and what he would die for if he had too. He had the patience of a man savoring the sweet taste of victory and wantin' it to last forever. And he had the patience of the hunter who knows that sooner or later every man and every beast makes a mistake. And his eyes gleamed in the sun while he waited for me to make the mistake that would open the way to send his blade tearing through my flesh and bones.

For me the fight was a thing in the way. A thing I had to do so I might get on to more important things. I had no time to give to the satisfaction of his revenge. At any minute the opportunity to rescue Annie might come and go. And how could I ever ease my own mind with a story of being too busy to go to her aid, even if I was busy fightin' for my life?

Ragged breath burned in my chest as the sun worked its way farther to the west. Every gulp of air was precious. I gulped at it like a dying man with a drink of water, but the air itself burned my lungs and left me gasping for another, cooler, breath.

A trickle of blood dripped from the Comanche's chin. It seeped from a scalp wound made when my knife found his head a little slow in dartin' away. The wound was nothin', but if the blood continued to flow, I knew the Indian's patience would do no good. Later, if not sooner, the strength of the man would flow with the blood. He would weaken and his hand would lower and my knife would find its way to his heart.

The only trouble was, I was also losin' blood on the sand. His knife slashed deep into the flesh of my left shoulder and my life was flowing steadily out, dripping uselessly from my finger tips.

There were no bells to signal the end of a round, and no seconds to patch up our wounds. The fight grew desperate for me. To lose was more than to die. It was to let Annie, and probably Preacher, die too. For if Preacher moved to rescue the girl he would count on me backing him up. Being ready with horse or gun or both, to keep him from falling victim to the Indians.

The time to jab and poke and watch for an opening was gone. Like a man gone wild, I swung my blade in great chopping arcs that cut the air in front of the Indian. He was so surprised by my sudden fury that he stepped back a little too far, a little too fast. His heel caught on a cactus and his arms flew up to catch his balance.

My blade cut a rib on his left side and crossed his body leaving a downward gash. His guts spilled out into his own hands. He stood lookin' at me, trying to push the life back into his body and knowin' he was dead.

If he had been a horse or a dog, torn in a fight with a lion or bear, I could easily have put him out of his misery. But he was a man. One of the bravest and truest men I had ever known, a man I would much rather have called friend than enemy. Even there, with the bloody knife still in my hand, I wished I could call back that fatal thrust. Surely, somehow I could have left him alive. I could have taken the knife from him and left him on the prairie. But I knew it wasn't so. To have left him alive would be to fight him another time.

I washed my wounded shoulder with the whisky I carried in my pack. Then I bound it tight with strips from my spare shirt. Only then did I turn back to the Indian.

There was no hate in his eyes, only sorrow that he had failed his people. I drank deep from my canteen. The water was good, but it could not wash the taste from my mouth. It was all so useless. And the taste was bitter. I helped Standing Bear hold the canteen to his lips. He sipped at the water as daintily as a lady at a fancy tea party. I reckon he was beyond talkin' 'cause he never uttered a word. But his eyes talked to me. Or maybe I just imagined the "thank you" I saw in them.

I left the canteen and the whisky beside him. It didn't take long to find the knife where he had dropped it in the sand. I hated myself for not having the courage to put the man out of his misery. I put the knife in his hand and turned away.

I couldn't help lookin' back from the top of the hill. The Other One raised the bottle toward me, then tilted his head back and drank.

"Just a damn whisky-drinkin' Indian," I told myself. But I couldn't explain the stinging in the corners of my eyes.

17

Rescue

The sun told me the fight lasted nearly two hours. My tortured body argued that it must have been closer to two days. Expectin' the Indians to be far to the Northwest, I spurred my pony to make up lost time. I let the animal run for a mile or more before the stupidity of the thing soaked in. In a land as hostile as the Llano, a man who killed his horse killed himself. And a man who took another man's| horse took his life. That's why they hung horse thieves. A horse was more than property to a man. The animal was life itself. And you don't go around takin' other folks lives, at least not without figurin' to pay the price.

The Kiowa had set up camp by the time I caught up with them. There was still enough light to see good, but I wasn't sure I believed what I saw. There was Preacher, big as life, right in among those Indians dickerin' away with them. No, I couldn't hear his words, but it ain't hard to tell when folks is arguin' by the way they wave their arms around in each other's face and such.

And I could see Annie. She was standin' by watchin' Preacher's ravin'! And she still held the infant son of Standing Bear. The baby was either asleep or takin' things in stride, 'cause he wasn't doin' any hollerin' or anything. Not like his daddy, I thought. That buck wouldn't let no chance for an argument get by without gettin' in the middle of it.

The Kiowa were camped at the bottom of a deep draw. The Staked Plains were cut by dozens of similar draws or creeks. But lookin' out across the plains, a man couldn't see the draws and arroyos that drained the plains when the flash floods came upon the land. All he could see was miles of nothing but more miles.

From where I lay hidden at the top of the draw, I could see a dozen or more pockets of water. Rains somewhere out on the prairie had filled the normally dry stream and the flowing water left behind it full "tanks" where the dirt was washed away from bedrock. The water in the tanks was clear and pure and fresh. The camp the Indians made was more permanent than they usually made—though the only permanent thing in their lives was moving. The fresh water drew the pronghorn antelope and the stragglers of the buffalo herds. While the hunting was good and the water was fresh, I knew the Indians would be in no hurry to leave.

But I was. I wanted Annie and Preacher out of that camp. I wanted to know they were safe and free and that it was all over. And I wanted to rest. It seemed like years since I had laid down to sleep without wonderin' if I would wake up dead. And it seemed like days since I had even slept at all. I was scared almost even to blink for fear my eyes would refuse to open again if I did.

When I woke up the sun was long gone and the moon was high in the sky. It didn't seem possible that I could have fallen asleep like I did. But I reckon the long day's ride and the fight and the bleedin' took more out of me than I knew. Anyway, I slept. I remembered hearin' stories of soldiers bein' shot for fallin' asleep on guard duty. Well, I figured if ever a guard needed to be shot, it was me. When the lives of the two people I cared more about than anything else in the world were on the line, I slept.

If I had some silly notion of slippin' into the camp and rescuin' Preacher and Annie during the night, my "nap" ended that. There were twenty or more lodges in the camp and I had no idea which held Annie or Preacher, if they weren't staked out on an anthill somewhere already. All I could do was to wait for morning, then probably for night to come again.

About the only thing left for me to do was to tend my horse. I led the animal downstream from the camp a good distance before I dared drop over the rim and make my way to the bottom of the draw. It didn't take long to find a water hole once we reached the bottom. I let my horse drink all I dared, then led him away from the water. He wasn't any too anxious to go, but I couldn't afford for him to get a water belly and founder on me.

While the horse grazed, I stripped the saddle and blanket from his back and rubbed him down with dry grass. I knew he wouldn't go far from the water, so I turned him loose and let him roll. He was one glad pony to be shed of that saddle. By the time he finished his roll, I figured it was okay to let him have some more water, so I didn't try to stop him when he headed back to the tank. The last thing I wanted was to chase a horse all over the prairie, so I slipped my stake rope around his neck while he drank. I drove the pin in the ground where the horse could get both water and grass.

I left the horse staked out and went for a closer look at the Indians. They had too many guards and dogs for me to get very close, so I held back and looked the situation over the best I could. It was a while before I missed the horses, and a while longer before I puzzled out where they might have gone. Their tracks chewed up the ground all around. As luck would have it, I had somehow managed to work my way between the Indians and their horse herd.

At last there was hope.

My fingers trembled a little while I saddled my horse. It was excitement, though, not fear that was giving me trouble. I swung into the saddle and went horse huntin'.

The guards who held the herd were both boys, not over twelve or fourteen years old. I wasn't much of an Indian, but I didn't have any trouble sneaking up on them. Most likely it was because they were both good sound sleepers.

When I saw the guards were only boys, my plan nearly fell apart. I sorely needed to knock them out, even kill them to get that herd of horses. I worried with it as long as I dared before I made up my mind. I hated to do it, but my plan was mostly bluff, so I couldn't let them see that I was alone. I slipped in on the back side of one of the sleeping boys and rolled him over on his belly before he could get his eyes open. I blindfolded him and tied his hands behind his back. The other boy woke up in all the commotion, but not soon enough to do any more than set back and let me tie and gag him. I was bettin' a lot on the boy I had blindfolded not seein' me, but I couldn't bring myself to knock a kid in the head.

I sorted Preacher's mule out of the herd and tied the first boy on his back. Then I drove the whole herd another five or six miles down the draw and scattered them as much as I could.

I hid the boy that had seen me in some brush, knowin' it wouldn't take a lot of lookin' to find him. I just hoped nobody found him too soon.

When I had the horses and the second boy safely

tucked away, I drove Preacher's mule, with the boy still on his back, right down the middle of the Kiowa camp. It was daylight by then and before we got more than a little ways in the camp we were surrounded by Indians and every one a-reachin' to pull me from my mount. I wasn't wantin' none of that, so I slipped my Colt from its holster and cocked the hammer. They backed off, but you could tell easy enough they wasn't givin' up. They meant to have my hide, but figured they could get it without losin' any braves. They were wrong.

"Does anybody speak English?" I asked loud enough to carry over the noise.

"I speak a mite of English." The voice came from behind me and sounded like the herald angels singing. It was Preacher.

"Can you talk to them?" I asked.

"Just a little. But they know sign language."

"Can you make them understand me."

"Sure, I can translate."

"Good. Tell them I have twenty men out on the plains."

I waited while Preacher made the signs and grunted some words I couldn't understand.

"Tell them my men have all their horses and the other boy."

A murmur ran through the crowd as they read Preacher's signs. Only the cocked pistol kept them from crushing me.

"I will trade the boy and the horses for the while woman and her baby."

The Indian boy was surrounded by questioning elders. He nodded and pointed and made signs. From time to time, he pointed at me and in the direction the horses had gone. I didn't know what he was sayin', but they were gettin' an earful.

You can guess my surprise when one old chief stepped out of the crowd and asked why I had come as an enemy into their camp.

"I am not your enemy," I said, "but you have taken my woman and I will have her back or there will be weeping in many lodges."

"You came in the night with your guns and your knives. You left many squaws without men and many men without squaws. You killed our children and or aged ones. And still you say you have not been our enemy."

"I have fought the Comanche," I said. "And the Indians of the East. But never have I fought the Kiowa."

"When have you fought the Comanche?" he asked.

"Many moons ago I fought them at the place where the ground raises up to the sky. I killed many. And many more went away to lick their wounds."

He looked at me in a new and strange way. "What do they call you?"

"My name is Laliker."

An excited whisper ran through the crowd as the old man muttered the words, "*Loco Diablo Blanco.* You are the white devil the Comanches sing about around their fires. It is your medicine that has weakened our enemies. Give us our boy and our horses, then take what is yours and go. We would not harm the enemy of Standing Bear."

"Standing Bear is dead." I told them of the fight on the prairie and how bravely Standing Bear had died. And they were proud to have fought so fine an enemy.

We parleyed then on more friendly grounds and I told them where to find the boy and the horses. I expect any gambler would call me a fool for showin' my hole card so soon, but I trusted that old chief.

They let us ride out easy enough, but I reckon they-changed their minds later. We were two hours from the camp when we heard them comin' behind us. There weren't more than four or five of them and it could be they were just some renegades that didn't share the old chief's idea of makin' peace with us.

Anyway, peace wasn't what they had on their minds. They came with bows firin' as fast as they could reload. On horseback a bow and arrow had it all over a muzzle loadin' rifle.

Annie was hard pressed to ride all out like that, holdin' the baby and all, but she was champion all the way. She never let her pony miss a stride and even managed to help Preacher drive the little pinto mare the chief had given her for milk for the baby.

I had enjoyed just about all the Indian trouble I wanted and was tryin' my best to keep from killin' any of them. But I had to fire toward them often enough to hold them back, just out of good bow range. They had about decided I wasn't too hot with my pistol and were startin' to close in. I dreaded the thought of creatin' more enemies like Standing Bear, but it was time to get down to some serious shootin'.

I took aim on the closest one and was about to send him huntin' in a happier place when they suddenly set their ponies on their heels. Preacher had been tryin' from the first time I laid eyes on him to sell me on the idea of miracles. Well, he just about did it then, 'cause how else could a man explain Estavan and Joe Baxter standin' there on that ridge throwin' lead after those Indians? The Indians weren't stickin' around, though, to play target.

By the time we topped the ridge, Estavan was on his mule. Baxter swung up on the little mare his sister was herdin' and we never missed a step.

18

Back From the Llano

Like we figured, Dominguez was already at Sam's wagon by the time we reached it. What we didn't figure on was Henry Tucker. Preacher and Estavan left him with the posse headin' toward Mexico. Tucker wasn't sayin' much about how he came to be wanderin' around on foot so far from where they split up. Fact is, he wasn't sayin' much about anything. And what he was sayin' didn't make enough sense to sort out the truth from the things his sick mind made up.

Tucker was in about as bad a shape as a man could get in and still claim to be alive. It was hard to believe a man could survive in the condition he was in. But the will to live is sometimes stronger in a man than any amount of reason would let us believe. Or maybe it's the fear of death.

"He came a staggerin' in here two days ago," Sam said. "He was naked plumb down to that Kiowa breech cloth he was wearin'. Most of his hide was burned off by the sun. That sandstorm nearly blinded him. Might have. I ain't got enough sense out of him to tell much about how he's doin'."

I never had much use for Tucker, myself, but I wouldn't wish what he had gone through on any man or dog. Preacher says there's a God in Heaven, and

151

I figure he's right. Anyway, if there is and if he made a Hell, he surely used the Llano Estacado for a pattern. If ever a man came back from Hell, it was Tucker. Even a day in that land without a hat or horse, without water or even clothes would kill most men. And we had no idea how many days Tucker wandered around out there like that. It was a thing to ponder on a winter day when there wasn't much to do but sit around the fire and think. But until we got back to the settlements there wasn't time to take on any unnecessasary worrin'.

I let Sam and Dominguez worry about tendin' Tucker. Joe Baxter and Estavan scouted our trail and kept us goin' the easiest route east. Of course, by then we had made enough trips to almost have a road worn in the dirt from Dallas to the caprock. At least an easy trail. Anyway, Estavan took the lead and kept us from runnin' into any trouble. Preacher remembered those Kiowas that tried to go back on the promise their chief made about us goin' in peace. He rode our back trail.

For me, there wasn't but one important thing left to do. That was gettin' Annie Baxter back home.

"What will the people say?"

Her question came at me out of the clear blue and I wasn't sure what she was thinkin' about. Annie insisted on ridin' horseback, though there was plenty of room on Sam's wagon. I tried to get her to at least put the baby on the wagon, but she wouldn't be separated from it. There was an understandin' between us, though. It seemed as natural as the sun risin' that we should ride side by side ahead of the wagon. We rode that way for days, side by side and both feelin' a deepdown peace that neither had ever known before. There were a thousand things we could have talked about, but for the most part we just rode. I was content in knowin' she was safe. And I knew that no person,

152

man or woman, could go through what she had been through without it makin' a different person out of them.

I mean, a person's hatreds and loves, their prejudices and their tolerances, their fears and their courage will either grow or wither away. And inside the person is the thing we call character. It's the thing that, if it's strong enough, keeps the hates and fears and prejudices from takin' over and completely ownin' a person. Some folks, like Tucker, couldn't stand up to their own hatreds. And there ain't a preacher or teacher or doctor that can help a man that's givin' his soul to his fears.

But Annie wasn't Tucker. She seemed almost indifferent toward the Indian who had taken her from her home and all the things she had known. If she prejudged the Indians who wandered through the land, and if she feared or hated them, it was not her prejudices, fears and hatreds that grew on the Llano.

She couldn't hate Indians and love the baby she held in her arms. Nor could she love the child and hate its father. She had faced her fears and came through with her head held high, with her back straight and her shoulders square. She had the pride and dignity that cannot be conquered by the unfortunate happenings of time or place.

But as we made our way eastward she faced new fears. There would be talk. Sharp tongued women with vile imaginations would say she had sold her body for easy treatment by Standing Bear. She would be shamed by those who vowed they would take their own lives before they submitted to any Indian. And many men would look upon her as one who had given herself to an Indian and would expect her to be loose and easy with her body.

In that time and land, where there was no money

153

or material goods, a woman's most prized possession was her name. To have her name raped by the gossip of those she had called friends was more fearsome to her than the rape of her body. How could I answer her question?

"I reckon they'll be glad to have you home and safe," was the best answer I could come up with. Even to me it sounded hollow and without much conviction.

"Some will," she said. "Like a few of Ma's friends. But you know how tongues wag. And I've seen the way men look at women who have escaped from the Indians."

"But you said the Comanche didn't touch you," I argued.

"It won't make any difference. As long as there aren't any true stories to get in the way, they can have more fun making up stories of their own." She sounded more bitter than I had ever heard her before.

"What are you going to tell them?" I asked the question but I feared the answer.

"Nothing. I'll keep my head high and let them think what ever they want to." Her jaw was set so tight the muscles bunched on the sides. She stared straight ahead, but she couldn't hide the flicker of fear in her eyes.

"It seems you ought to at least tell them Standing Bear never hurt you." I knew people as well as she did, and I knew how useless my argument was.

"I'll tell that, all right. But just to a few of Ma's old friends. And some of my closest friends. I guess I owe Ma's memory the respect of trusting her friends. Most of them have treated me like family since she died. But I won't give the gossips the satisfaction of denying any rumors."

A tear moistened the corner of her eye as she added,

"I won't know what to do if the men act like I'm something dirty."

"Let me know the first time any man gets out of line. I'll see it don't happen again." I guess I sounded a little foolish.

"What would you do? Shoot him? Or beat him senseless? And what favors do you think they would say I was doing for you? No, thank you!"

I knew she was frustrated in the seeming hopelessness of her problem. But the scorn in her words stung more than I wanted to admit. In fact, just about everything about her bothered me more than I wanted to admit.

"We could go away," I said. "Back to Missouri, or South to the coast. Or even out to Santa Fe."

Her face twisted into a mask of disgust. "No!" she almost screamed. "I expected some of the men to think I might do such a thing, but not you."

She lashed her horse into a fast trot and left me settin' with my teeth in my mouth and egg on my face. Surely, I wondered, she knew I was proposing to her?

Annie avoided me the rest of the day. Come supper time she filled a plate from Sam's bean pot and brought it to me. She handed me the beans and a cup of coffee and turned away without speaking. She wouldn't answer when I called to her. I wouldn't beg.

The camp was asleep, except I was on sentry. We still didn't trust the Indians. Annie came to me. Her chin hung on her breast and she wouldn't look me in the eye.

"I know how much I owe you," she said. "The others would never have found me if it had not been for you. Whatever you want of me is yours."

There was no mistakin' what she offered. The blood pounded hot in my veins. I wanted to grab and be consumed in the fulfillment of the moment. But I wanted more. I wanted everything love between a man and woman should be. And I couldn't have it, at least not yet. If I asked her to marry me she would accept and I would forever wonder if her only reason was a feeling that she owed it to me. I wanted a better relationship than that to base my marriage on.

"You know about men," I said to her, "so you know what is inside me right now. You better get back to bed before I lose control of myself."

There were tears on her cheeks when she raised her face to meet mine. "Whatever you want," she said. She didn't leave.

"This afternoon, in my clumsy way, I tried to ask you to marry me. I know what you thought I was asking for, but you were wrong. I also know how bad a job I made of the whole thing. There's never been anything said or done between us to make you want to marry me. If you'll allow it, when we get back to the settlements, I'll call on you like's fittin' and proper. I want no more misunderstandings between us. You can assure yourself that my intentions have been nothing but honorable. It's true, of course, that I have the same needs as any other man, but I want more than a night in the prairie grass."

I had practiced that speech in my mind all afternoon, hoping to get a chance to explain to her. If she had interrupted, I would never have finished it. But all the time I was goin' on, she stood meek as a lamb and just listened.

Finaly she raised her eyes to mine again. Her tears still glistened in the moonlight and shame burned her face. "Will you hate me because of tonight?"

"Myself, maybe, but never you," I answered.

"Do you still want to marry me?"

"Yes, but I won't ask you until I can be sure you

want me as much as I want you. I don't want a wife bought in a fight that cost a brave man his life.''

Her body pressed against mine as she kissed me good night. The promises it made tempted me almost more than I could resist. But she wasn't the kind of woman for a roll in the hay. She was a good woman, the kind a man marries, the kind you don't take advantage of in a moment of weakness, either yours or hers.

I watched Annie cross the camp to Sam's cook tent, the one we set up every night for her and the baby. The silver light of the moon bounced off her hair like a halo you see in those old-time paintings in churches and such. That didn't do a whole lot to straighten out the mixed-up feelin's inside me.

The rest of the way home, Annie kept a respectable distance between us. But there were moments when our fingers touched or when our eyes met when we would linger to suffer the agonies of unfulfilled love. If I hadn't already promised her a proper courtship, I would have asked her again to marry me on the trail. After all, we had her brother along to give consent and Preacher to do the honors. But even on the frontier a woman had a need for being courted, though time didn't often allow for the long courtships that were fashionable in the East. And if she came back from captivity with a husband, the gossips would have more than enough to keep them guessing for months.

Aside from me moonin' over Annie, the only problem we had on the way home was Tucker. He was able to set a horse long before we got back to Dallas. He passed back and forth among us like he was sizin' us up. He wasn't sayin' any more about how he came to be wanderin' around on the Llano like he was. Fact is, he was sayin' less. And he kept askin' questions about what he might have said while he was out of his head. A lot of his questions hinted at the true answers, at least to the truth he wanted to keep hidden from the world. It didn't take a real smart person to add up all the things that were botherin' the man. The old Kiowa chief had told us about the massacre and about the one who followed, killing his people in the night. I had no proof but I was sure in my mind that the evil could be laid at the feet of Tucker.

I made an effort to keep the man in sight for the rest of the journey. But sometimes I would feel an uneasy tingle on the back of my neck and would turn to see Tucker starin' at me like a vulture waiting to be sure the carcass is dead. I saw Preacher and Estavan watching Tucker, too, so I knew they shared my suspicions, if not my fears of the man. We had nothin' but our suspicions so we never discussed the situation. It would have been a lot easier on me if we had taken it on ourselves to arrest him and turn him over to the army.

19

Major Arnold

The word went ahead of us as we made our way into the little town of Dallas. The single street filled with people, curious to see the girl returned from captivity, and the Indian child she carried. Several who had ridden with the posse stood among the curious. They looked stern-faced at the girl but would not look us in the eye. As we rode abreast of them, they turned, one by one, and made their way away from the crowds.

It was plain they were shamed by the return of the girl. If they had listened to Preacher and Estavan, they would have been in on the rescue. Instead they had followed Tucker and came back with a story of a great battle in which they won victory over the Indians who took Annie. They told of her death at the hands of the Kiowa and how the Indians had ambushed them. The return of Preacher and Estavan with the Baxters made a lie out of their story. I felt an uneasy stir in the air. Makin' liars of men was one sure way to make trouble.

Joe Baxter claimed the privilege of taking his sister home alone. I told him of my intentions to come calling, but yielded to his request that I wait a few days to let her rest. He seemed real taken with the idea of someone askin' his permission to call on Annie. I didn't see need to mention that I would come whether it suited him or not. But I couldn't deny Annie's need of time to rest and collect her wits.

Preacher and Estavan went to the meetin' hall to make ready for the next day's services, it bein' Saturday when we made it back. Precious few Sundays slipped by without Preacher holdin' some kind of services. Even out on the plains, he insisted on stopping the wagons long enough to remember the day and its Creator. But among his flock he became a different man. He took on a softer look around his eyes and his hands seemed more natural closed around the tiny hand of a child than around the stock of a rifle.

Sam and Dominguez took the wagon and extra stock on back to our camp on the Trinity. They carried the burden of telling the rest of the teamsters about the death of O'Leary. He was a friend to all of us and the news of the rescue would only help a little to ease the empty place he left.

Left alone, I was without purpose of destination. The finish of the job didn't bring a desire to celebrate. The job we had handled was more one to cause a man to seek home and family than one to send him in search of liquor and loud crowds. The closest thing I had to a home was the little group of wagons camped on the bank of the Trinity. But there was nothing homelike about the wagons. They did not draw me like a home draws a man. Instead I was pulled toward the Baxter ranch. And I had never even seen the place.

I knew my men. By now the wagons would be empty, and the goods we hauled from the coast sold for the best available price. The mules would be grazed and grained and in prime shape for another drive to whatever destination we chose for them. For a teamster, there were no profits in a parked wagon. The men would be expecting to hit the trail by first light. And I owed it to my partner, Luke McClure. The wagons

160

were three parts his and only one part mine. To keep them idle was to cheat him out of his rightful profits. And they had already set idle for weeks I hadn't bothered to count. Not that Luke would have hesitated to do the same as I had done.

But I had chosen a woman and declared my intentions. To ride away and leave her to wonder if I would keep my promise to come calling would be to insult her womanhood. I faced the same problems faced by man ever since he laid down his club and chose to court the favors of women instead of taking them by force.

It was clear that my responsibilities dictated I should roll my wagons. What I needed was an excuse to stick around at least long enough to see Annie a few times. I worried the thing around in my mind but I didn't have a lot of luck. The best idea I could come up with was to gather what cargo I could and send it back to Missouri. There wasn't much to gather, maybe half a load of cow hides and a few beaver skins Tailor had traded some trapper out of down at the Mercantile.

There wasn't a family in the settlements that didn't need some hard money, but there just weren't any cash crops. Save the seed and there wasn't enough wheat or corn in all of Peter's Colony to load one of my Conestogas. And if we got wheat to Missouri, chances were we would have to feed it to our own mules. The markets for commodities like that were good in the East, but it would cost a fortune to freight wheat from Missouri to the seaboard.

I could see the time coming when there would be great trains of wagons hauling the commodities of the plains south to the coast to be loaded onto ships bound for ports all over the world. But not yet. Those times would come when there were more people and more

161

plows, when the plains were gentled and tamed and yielded to the caressing hand of the farmer.

For the time being, there was little to do but build foundations. I had wagons ready and waiting for their cargos. And Manuel Sainz was building our mercantile and warehouses and graineries on the coast. We had a lot of things going for us. McClure's knowledge of the freighting business and Sainz's influence with the Mexican people made good partners for my hard-headed stubbornness. But most of all we had a quarter ton of Indian silver we hauled out of New Mexico that set us up with the best stock and rigging in the state.

All of that didn't help me with my problem at hand. I needed goods to load my wagons and a trip to send them on that could be handled without me going along. A trip to Missouri would buy me sixty days. Time enough for courtin' and marryin'. Or time enough for Annie to marry someone else if I was gone with the wagons.

I was settin' in the shade of the bank worryin' on all of these things and not much aware of what was goin' on around me. I don't know how long the army private stood there before he got my attention.

"Mr. Laliker?"

I looked around at him and was startled at how young he was. I was only twenty-four myself, but felt old in the ways of things in that rugged land. The private might have been seventeen or twenty-seven, but his eyes carried the innocent look of one who has never had to make a life and death decision, one who has never had to decide whether to kill or risk death himself. It made me feel old and used up to think of the times my hand had grasped the butt of my Colt while other men's lives flowed into the sand. And the Other One, Standing Bear, who died; I grieved that

I'd had to kill him but I was satisfied that he had spent his life for the purchase of honor.

"What can I do for you, boy?"

The young man's face reddened at my careless use of the term, "boy." As with most young men, myself included, the use of the word said the speaker considered himself superior to the other. I bit my lip and silently vowed to make up for my slip if given the chance.

"Major Arnold wants to see you, sir. At Camp Worth. He says it's important and you should come right away."

I wasn't used to bein' ordered around by any man. I expect I had spent enough time with my mules to pick up some of their stubbornness, too. Anyway, I bristled a little at the thought of some army major sending for me like I was one of his soldiers.

"You ride on back and tell your Major Arnold I said I was too busy to ride down there. If he wants to see me, he can come up here."

"But, sir, I've been waiting a week. I've been camped out at your wagons. Major Arnold said I should bring you back with me."

I felt kind of sorry for the private. And sorry I had snapped off my decision based on pride instead of sense. I could ride to the post and back in less than two days and tend to whatever business the Major had for me with time to spare. It wouldn't break McClure or me for the wagons to set that much longer. But I wasn't in a mood for any more interruptions in my plans. I turned my back on the soldier and started to walk away.

"Sorry about that," I said. "We've all got our problems. I guess you'll just have to . . ." That's as far as I got. When I heard the revolver cock I froze in my tracks.

"You don't understand, Mr. Laliker. I was ordered to bring you back and I will."

I turned to face the man I had mistaken for a boy. You bet a sixgun can make a man out of a boy. The quiver I heard in his voice was in his eyes, too. The private knew my name and he knew my reputation. He knew I could kill him where he stood before he could get off even one shot. He knew the choice of whether he lived or died was in my hands. But he had a duty and was willing to die to see it through. I never saw a braver thing in my life, though I've seen lots of good men die well.

I pretended to be unaware of the gun the youth held. "Did your Major say why he wants to see me?"

"No sir. Not to me. But I heard him and Sergeant Wilkins talkin' about a shipload of supplies and weapons layin' somewhere on the coast. I think he wants to hire your wagons to freight them to the camp."

"All right," I said. "You ride back to the post. Tell your Major I'll be there by noon tomorrow. Tell him I have a man, Manuel Sainz, in Galveston. We have warehouses and docks. Your ship can offload there and be on its way. If you're right about the cargo, tell Major Arnold to go ahead and make contact with the ship. I'll strike a fair bargain with him on the rate."

The soldier looked at me almost like he was hungry to take me at my word. The barrel of his pistol drooped and his thumb relaxed on the hammer.

"A freighter don't eat very good with his wagons settin' empty," I said. "Be sure your major gets the message right. 'Unload the ship at Manual Sainz Docks in Galveston.' Do I need to send a written order or will he take your word?"

The pistol slid back into its holster and the young private was visibly relieved by my refusal to acknowledge the presence of the weapon. ''I won't need the note. We'll look for you before noon.'' He didn't need words to say he would come after me if I didn't do as I said I would. I admired the spirit in his voice and there was a hint of knowing in his eyes I had missed before. Or maybe he grew some in realizing he was man enough to stand up despite his fear.

There wasn't much nonsense about Major Arnold. He knew his job and intended to see to it that no wool was pulled over his eyes. I quoted him a rate for hauling his goods and was amazed at his answer. ''I want those goods delivered here. I was told you had good men. I count good men as bein' the most important asset a man can have. It don't make any difference whether he's a businessman or a soldier. They also say you have good wagons and good teams. How can you figure to make a profit and haul for a dollar a ton to the mile?''

''There'll soon be other freighters workin' this area,'' I told him. ''When that time comes, I don't want to be remembered as the man that cheated his customers to make a quick profit while there was no competition. Barring the kind of troubles a man can't figure on, I can turn a fair profit at the rate I quoted.''

''I'll tell you what, Laliker,'' he said. ''This country needs men willin' to take a risk. I need you now, and I'll need you again. I want to be sure you'll still be here when I do. The goin' rate the government is payin' is a dollar fifty per ton mile. We'll draw up a contract at a dollar twenty-five. That'll give you a margin and still make the brass think I drove a hard bargain. I'll send Segeant Lane with a five-man escort for your wagons. When will you be ready to leave?''

''My men pulled out at daylight. Runnin' empty like they are, they'll make thirty miles by dark. If your sergeant hurries he might catch up to them by the time they reach Calveston.''

''Private Reed told me you pumped him for information. You took quite a risk sending your wagons on the strength of what he overheard between Sergeant Wilkins and myself.''

''I guess you might say so,'' I answered. ''But the wagons couldn't set any longer. South was as good as any direction to send them. I was willing to gamble on Sainz rounding us up a cargo if Reed was wrong.''

With our business tended, Major Arnold turned the conversation to other matters.

''What can you tell me about the trouble with the Kiowa you've been having over your way?''

Now what I knew about the Kiowa incident and what I thought I knew weren't necessasarily the same thing. I had Tucker's story about bein' ambushed by the Indians and the stories of the rest of the posse seemed to back him up. Anyway, they all agreed that the Kiowa had ambushed them and they had to fight their way out of quite a mess. I told that version of things to Major Arnold and went on to tell him about Standing Bear and our fight on the Llano.

''That's pretty much the same story I got out of the men,'' he said. ''Except they said they were sure it was the same bunch of Indians that had taken the girl and that she was dead.''

''They were probably doin' a little raidin' aground all right,'' I said. ''But the Comanche took Annie. To the best of my knowledge those Kiowa were as inocent as babies. At least to hear the old chief tell it, they were.''

He sat straight up and demanded, ''What old chief?''

I told him about the Kiowa findin' Annie after the sand storm and how we managed to rescue her from them. Then I repeated the Indin's version of the massacre. "It's likely he was lyin' thought," I said. "He didn't have much to gain by braggin' about ambushin' a posse of white men."

"He wouldn't," Arnold agreed. "But he may have been telling the truth. My patrol came across the battle site two days too late. The Indians evidently came back for their dead, 'cause there wasn't but one body in the camp. But my scout says the Indians were ambushed by about twenty white men. He claims the attack came at night and the Kiowa were slaughtered in their sleep. More than half the tribe was wiped out. I don't know how much he was makin' up and how much he read from the sign in the tracks, but he claims there were as many women and children killed as men."

"Who was scoutin' for you?" I asked the question, not really figurin' on knowin' the man.

"A Mexican by the name of Ramirez. Seems to know his work as well as any, but he could be just tryin' to stir up trouble between the settlers and the army. I understand there's a lot of Mexicans that would like to see Texas under the Mexican flag again."

"Not Ramirez," I said. "He pulled me through hell and high water and even saved my bacon from a Mexican prison. If he says it was a massacre, you can bet on it."

"I've been afraid of this all along," Arnold said. "Part of my job is to arrest and bring to trial any white man that commits a crime against the Indians. But I can't arrest twenty men. What would their families do without them? What would any of the people do with half the men gone from the settlements?"

"You can't arrest them all, that's for sure. But you can get the leader. The whole idea behind the move to protect the Indians is more of a roundabout way of protecting the whites by preventing trouble than anything else. I doubt that your superiors ever meant for you to jail half of the men in this area.''

He didn't look convinced, so I took a different tack. ''Those are good people. They would never have thought of such a thing if they hadn't been led by a warped mind.''

I told him of Preacher's account of the struggle for leadership in the posse and of Tucker's blind hate for all Indians. He went a little pale when I described the mutilated corpses and the living dead that had been laid at the door of Tucker since the return of Irene. And I told him the details of the old Kiowa chief's account of the massacre and of the one who followed his people out onto the Llano and entered their camps in the night.

''He must be insane,'' Arnold said. ''He's got to be stopped before he starts a war with half the Indian tribes in the country.''

''At least I can get you a witness,'' I said. ''There was one man with him we can count on. He wouldn't have followed Tucker in a thing like that under any circumstances. Ortiz is his name. I'll look him up and get his story. If he tells it like I think he will, you won't have any trouble gettin' all the witnesses you want. They'll quit Tucker like rats off a sinkin' ship.''

The look on Arnold's face told the story before he could speak the words. ''I told you we only found one body. What I didn't get around to saying was that the body wasn't an Indian. It was your friend Ortiz. He was shot in the back of the head from close range. His pistol was still in the holster. Ramirez says the Kiowa would have taken it if he had used it against them. It was still loaded.''

That bein' the first I heard about Ortiz dyin' in the

168

raid, I was set back. There was no doubt about his murderer. And it was me that brought him back from the hell he had been sentenced to on the Llano. Tucker.

20

Tucker

The homeward journey from the Llano strengthened
Tucker's body. Each day he felt the surge of power
flowing back into his cat-like muscles. And like a cat
he sat back, sleepy-eyed, waiting for his chance. From
the time his head cleared enough for him to recognize
his surroundings, he knew. These people would have
to die. There was no other way for any of them. The
baby was Indian and the girl was a lover of Indians.
Didn't the way she protected the child make her as
bad as they were? It was not natural for a white woman
to love an Indian baby so much.

And the man, Dominguez. His skin was too brown
to have much white blood flowing in his veins. He
was Indian. It made no difference that he carried a
Christian name and claimed Mexican decent. He was
Indian and would die like the others for what they did
to Irene.

Sam, the cook, was there all the time, tending him
through the ravings of his delirium. What might he
have said that Sam would repeat once they reached
civilization? It pained Tucker to think of killing the
one who had pulled him through. But Sam might know
of the massacre and of the ones Tucker had murdered

in the night. And if he told, Tucker knew he would die at the end of a rope.

And Preacher and Estavan. They knew he led the posse after they separated the group. If it was ever discovered that the massacre had occurred, there would be no question as to the leader who had brought about the carnage. And besides, Estavan was black. Darker than any Indian. A heathen worse than an Indian. Preacher would die for what he knew, but Estavan would die for the color of his skin.

It would be a shame to kill the Baxter boy. Joe was like him. He went out to rescue his sister from the Indians. He had brought back a woman turned Indian. In time, he would come to hate the redskins as much as Tucker did for what they had done to Annie. He could be a better ally than Bob Cooley. But to kill the girl, he must kill her brother. There wasn't time to wait until Baxter could see that Annie was dirty, contaminated by the Indians who had used her. She was now an Indian herself. Only an Indian could love another Indian the way she loved the baby she held constantly at her breast.

But mostly he must kill Laliker. There was a knowing in the way he looked at Tucker that made the man cringe in guilt. It was as though Laliker could see into his innermost thoughts. Like he knew of the massacre and of all the nights when his knife drank the blood of the red man.

But there was need to be careful. If one died and another lived, there would be danger. If any of the others died before Laliker, the man would come for him. He would come with pistols blazing and he wouldn't listen to any excuses. Because he would know. He could see inside Tucker's mind. Laliker must die first, and the others in their time.

Tucker watched the group split into its natural parts.

Baxter and his sister rode off toward their ranch. The sight of the baby the girl carried pulled at his warped mind. But he must wait. First Laliker.

Estavan and Preacher were soon gone. Everybody seemed to have forgotten him. When Sam and his wagon disappeared down the trail, Tucker had already slipped from sight. He hid himself in the shadows of the the general store and pondered the situation. There would be no better time to kill Laliker. He was alone and standing in plain view in front of the bank. One quick shot and it would be over—except for the people. Old John Brisco was sunning himself in front of the store. A shot would bring him into the alley on the run. And it would take another killing to shut his mouth.

The thought of killing the old man didn't bother Tucker, but there were those two old busybodies. The store keeper's wife, Mrs. Tailor, was standing twenty feet from Laliker, gossiping the day away with Mrs. Johnson. They showed no intention of letting up. Most likely, Tucker thought, they'll be there 'til dark. Carefully, he weighed the consequences of killing Brisco and the women. Too many, he thought. If I get Laliker on the first shot, I might get all three of them before they get to cover. But if I have to use two shots on Laliker, those old women will get a look at me and be in the bank before I can take care of Brisco and get any shots at them. I'll have to think of a better plan.

Tucker led his horse well away from the little settlement before he stopped. He slipped his rifle, the one Laliker had given him, from the saddle boot and climbed to the top of a slight rise. The shot would be from less than eighty yards with little risk of a miss, and no risk of being recognized.

The scene before him was almost as he left it. The women were still gossiping and Brisco was still sunning himself. Laliker had moved to a chair leaned against the front of the bank. He was in the shade, but his outline was visible against the light-colored stone walls of the building. The only thing missing was the darker shadow that had lurked among the shadows a few minutes before. But none of the people on the street had been aware of Tucker and none would be able to say who fired the shot.

Carefully the man studied the outline of the figure on the porch in front of the bank. A head shot would be the quickest, but it was too risky. The outline of Laliker's hat made it too hard to be sure of his shot. A body shot would be more sure. Even if he missed the heart, a lung or gut shot was just as fatal, though it might take days for his victim to die. But the body was a target hard to miss.

Tucker set the sights on the center of the shadowed outline. There was no breeze to allow for and the distance did not require holding high to allow for bullet drop. It was almost too easy. His finger took up the slack in the trigger. The slack was gone and the trigger was pushing back against his finger when the sights filled with blue.

"Damm!" Tucker swore, releasing the pressure on the trigger. "Where the hell did that soldier come from?"

Nobody answered but it didn't take long before Tucker remembered the military post newly established to the west and south of the settlement. "One of Arnold's soldiers," Tucker reasoned with himself. "There might be a bunch of them around."

He watched as the two men talked and tensed when Laliker left his chair and turned his back on the soldier. Excitement welled up in him when the man in blue took his postol from its holster and aimed it at the retreating back. The sights of his rifle again centered on Laliker. "Start something, dammitt," he told the distant figures. "Either one of you. I'll finish it."

Disappointed, he watched the soldier and Laliker ride off in different directions. Laliker didn't see the shadow that followed him to his encamped wagons and then away again toward Camp Worth.

21

Finish

Tucker was the army's problem, and the situation was in good hands. Major Arnold was a competent man, the kind who was determined to have the right of the situation before he went charging into battle. He set out to handle the Tucker mess like he would have any military campaign.

By the time I rode out of the camp, he already had a scout detail preparin' to head out onto the Llano looking for the old chief and his band of Kiowas. Though he had my version of the chief's view of the massacre, he wanted the old man to tell it himself in front of a jury. Neither one of us had much faith in his troops either findin' the Kiowa or convincin' him to come to the camp to testify in the White man's court. But accordin' to Arnold, even Tucker was entitled to have as much evidence as possible presented at his trial. And he had the right to face his accuser. I couldn't see the difference myself, but the major said no judge would let me tell the story like the Chief had told it to me.

At the same time, he had Lieutenant Craig preparin' to go after Preacher to get a list of all the members of the posse. With the names in hand, he figured he could question each man until he found one or more who would testify against Tucker. If he had been dealing with a gang of criminals, his job would have been close to impossible. But out of twenty honest men, we were sure there would be several anxious to clear their conscience.

By the time Major Arnold had his campaign laid out, it was past midafternoon. Since there seemed little reason to hurry, the soldiers decided to delay departure until morning. They invited me to spend the night at the camp and travel with them the next day, but I had my own reasons for wanting to get back as soon as possible.

It seemed like my problems had solved themselves. The wagons were rolling. For the first time since I tied up with McClure, we had a consignment of freight that would guarantee us a profit. And I had time on my hands. The trip would take at least three weeks, maybe six, depending on weather and luck. More likely it would be somewhere in between. Whichever, I had time to establish my claim on Annie Baxter.

It was three hours from sundown when I rode out of Camp Worth. My head was filled with all the things that twist up a man's thinkin' when a woman is involved. I wasn't one to ride blind down a trail, but all I was seein' that day was Annie—the way she cocked her eyes around to look at me and the way she hesitated when our fingers happened to touch, like she wanted to stretch the moment out. The way her eyes brightened when she looked up from what she was doing and discovered me watching her. And the promise that had been in her lips and her body as it pressed against mine in the only kiss we had shared. Things to muddle the mind.

But there was more to Annie than the flirty girl who first caught my eye. When a man chooses a horse, the first thing he looks for is staying power. The depth of chest and strength of muscle and limb that says the animal won't quit on you when the going gets rough. Annie was one to stay with. The way she took the Indian baby and made it a part of her, not just a job that had to be tended, let me know she was one that would accept what life dealt her. She didn't just tolerate life, but lived completely. And on the frontier a woman had to be a stayer. Life dealt some rough hands and women strong enough to keep tryin' despite all the hardships and failures were rare. Most gave up and were old women by thirty-five, with nothing to look forward too but a few more years of torture and maybe some of the rewards in Heaven Preacher talked of.

But not Annie. I could see in her the strength that would keep her spirit young through years of hardships and trials and frustrations. I could see her beside me in whatever life handed out, lending me her strength when I needed it and helping me to keep going when I was burdened beyond my ability to stand. I knew on the first day I met Annie that I could love her. Now I knew why.

The shot knocked Annie and everything else from my mind. It came from a great distance; the sound beat the bullet to me by the split second it took me to jerk my head around. The bullet took me in the side of the head and knocked me from my horse. If it hadn't been for the sound, or whatever instinct a man gains living on the frontier that caused me to turn my head, I would have been dead before I hit the ground. Instead I was down and hurt, but alive and wantin' to stay that way.

It never entered my mind that the hidden rifleman might be somebody besides Tucker. I had been around and knew some about people and if I had been thinkin', I would have known Tucker would come for me. He had to. Things were stackin' up too deep around him. Preacher and me tellin' our stories might or might not get him hung by the army. But if word was spread about how Ortiz died, Tucker wouldn't stand a chance. Even the men who rode with him on that night wouldn't put up with the murder of Ortiz.

Ortiz had been a good man, one who asked for nothing he didn't earn, yet would have given everything he owned to anyone who needed it worse than he did. He was a man who stood tall and walked proud in the way only a truly unselfish person can.

There were a dozen other reasons Tucker would want me dead, but right then, I didn't stop to take inventory. My most urgent problem was one of those "dammed if you do and dammed if you don't" propositions. If Tucker was watching and I moved, I was sure to draw another shot. But if I laid there out in the open, he might decide to just shoot me another time or two to make sure I was dead. I worried with it 'til I realized the problem was past. If he intended to shoot again, he wouldn't have waited so long. It seemed he would have shot my body to pieces then left me for the crows and coyotes if he could see me. There was too little for him to gain to take the chance of exposin' himself. Unless he hoped I wasn't dead and he could look me in the eye when he finished me. Or maybe he wanted to butcher me like he had done so many Indians.

Either way, I was still up the creek without a paddle. He knew exactly where I was, even if he couldn't see me. All he had to do was set tight and wait me out. If I moved, I would be a dead man. And if he could see me, he might be just lettin' me suffer before he finished me off.

There I was thinkin' again. Like I've said, the only times I get into trouble are when I go to thinkin'. All

I really knew was that he was out there somewhere hid in a million acres of scrub oak and mesquite thicket. Chances were slim of him leavin' without makin' sure I was dead. He was out there all right. And closer than I thought. I like to have come unglued and run away when he yelled at me from fifty feet or so away.

"Laliker! You just as well come on out from wherever you're hidin'. It won't do you no good."

I let it soak in for a while. He had moved in and lost my position. He didn't have any more idea where I was than I did him. Less. His voice gave him away. He was in easy pistol range. I was tempted to empty my Colt into the thicket where the voice came from. Odds were good I would catch him flat-footed and get a bullet into him. But they were a lot better that all I would shoot would be a lot of air and trees and ground.

Anyway, by the time I thought it over it was too late. Tucker was a moccasin man. He moved like the wind across the ground, leaving little track and making no sound. He could have been out of the thicket and another fifty feet away by the time I sorted out his location and argued with myself about whether or not to shoot.

I was still out in the open and not likin' it at all. Sooner or later Tucker would spot me and likely things would finish up real sudden for me. I just made up my mind to break for the brush when his voice froze me back in my place.

"Come on out. You don't have a chance this way. Sooner or later I'll find you and kill you. Come out and face me and let the best man win."

That was a temptin' offer. I knew of only one man who could match the spead of my hand and the accuracy of the pistol I wore. But Manual Sainz was in

Galveston. In a gun duel, I wouldn't have given much for Tucker's chance against me. And not much more with knives. In my fight with Standing Bear I learned fast about choppin' and thrustin', slashin' and slicin'. About jabbin' and blockin' and strainin' and holdin'. In that fight I learned about an instinct for survival deep within me that wouldn't let me quit as long as there was hope or breath or life left inside me. Even when I knew I was fightin' the other man's fight under his terms. Sure, I would gave gladly taken him on man to man, him choosin' the weapons.

Trouble was, he had already chosen the weapons and the time. The weapon was deceit and the time was whenever he first got a glimpse of me. I never figured him to think so low of me as to consider me a fool. He wouldn't expect me to step out to take up his offer, he was succeedin' in unnervin' me somethin' awful. Even knowin' he was doin' his dangdest to get me to show myself, I had a hard fight with my feet just keepin' them from cuttin' out for the closest mesquite thicket.

If it was just a matter of waitin' him out, I could have stood it a lot easier. But there was the wound on the side of my head to consider. I didn't have the foggiest notion about how bad it was. For all I knew the bullet was somewhere inside my head and I was already dead, but just too stubborn to admit it. Or I didn't have enough sense to know it.

From the first, I figured the pain would ease off, given a little time. But it hadn't. At least I don't think it had. That's one of the few blessings in life given out in equal measure to all people. Nobody can remember pain. We can remember joy and happiness and all the good things that happen to us, but not pain. Preacher swore we were made that way to keep us from goin' out of our minds any time we hurt ourselves. Said if we could remember pain, we would get to rememberin' every time we got hurt and the memories would be worse than the hurt and you can see where all of that would lead to if I kept on. The point is, I was hurtin' and not feelin' enough better to know it.

But more than the hurtin', I was scared of passin' out. I didn't want to wake up and find myself trussed up like a Christmas turkey with Tucker settin' there just a waitin' with his knife ready to slice me up and serve to the crows. And me watchin' the pieces bein' served.

Either he was farther off or he was in a low place, 'cause his voice kind of echoed the next time he hollered.

"Laliker! You ain't foolin' me none. I've seen a hundred men shot off their horses. I know the difference between a dead man and a live one!"

It was good to have a second opinion about my bein' alive, but I would have rather it was someone's besides Tucker's.

It was time. I would get no better chance to get to shelter. I rolled over and lunged toward the mesquite. I tried to get my feet under me, but they wouldn't go. It makes me ashamed to tell it, but I had to stop right there and toss my cookies. Man, I was sick. I lost everything they gave me to eat on the military base. I heaved 'til there wasn't nothin' left but dry heaves and the foul taste of soured acid and bile. That, and the sound of Tucker comin' on the run.

A man ought to be sure of his target before he fires a gun. There's been a dozen times as many men killed accidently by men that didn't take time to be sure of their targets than have ever been killed deliberately by men with guns. And I wasn't any exception. I sure

181

should have waited for sight of Tucker before I shot that old mossy-horned cow to pieces.

Well, she was comin' from where I expected Tucker and she wasn't waitin' on no one to invite her. I reckon she must have lost her calf and mistook the noise I was makin' for her baby callin'. Anyway, I emptied my Colt into her. She broke out of the brush just as I dropped the hammer on my last round, but it was too late to call it back.

I rolled for brush and got myself hid as quick as possible. By the time I was in the brush, I had the pin pulled and the cylinder for my Patterson Colt loose in my hand. It took a three count to drop my spare cylinder into place and another five to cap the nipples. I cocked the gun and looked up expecting to meet Tucker's bullet between my eyes.

There wasn't a sign or a sound from the man. It seemed clear he had missed his chance. For those brief seconds while my gun was empty, I was easy prey for an man with a gun out of knife range. He could have stepped in and shot me up worse than I did that cow. But then the Kiowa chief's words came back to me. Words about one who sneaked into the camp at night, so quietly that even the dogs were not disturbed. One who killed again and again so silently and so surely that people sleepin' in the same tepee were not awakened.

Tucker was a night stalker. The cow gave him my position and the threat of his rifle would keep me there, but he waited for the night. The hair crawled on the back of my neck thinkin' about facin' so skillful a stalker in the black of night. My hand moved to the butt of my knife and it was in my hand without thought. I tested its edge against my thumb and found it as razor sharp as when it spilled the life of Standing Bear onto the plains. I dropped the knife back into its holster, but I didn't loop the safety thong back over its grip. I might want that knife out in an awful hurry, I thought.

More than an hour passed with us locked in a Mexican stand-off. Flies buzzed around the drying blood of the dead cow. They must have sent out invitations to the feast to all their relatives for miles around. Anyway, they came by the thousands. As the carcass was completely covered, they spread out, looking for easier pickin's or shelter for the night. They swarmed over my sweaty face and across my hands in droves. I swore at them under my breath, but dared not try to shoo them away. In that game of hide-n'-seek, I sure didn't want to be tagged "it."

My hat might have covered the open wound on the side of my head, but it was gone, lost in the fall and left behind when I scrambled for cover. The flies worried with the bloody mess of flesh and blood that had been my head. Their buzz became a roar that drove me to the brink of comin' up screamin' and shootin' from my hidin' place. My mind made pictures of the biting flies boring into my torn flesh to lay their eggs, and millions of maggots workin' alive inside my head.

I couldn't help it. My hand wouldn't stay away. The risk of death was less threat to me than the thoughts that filled my tortured mind. I waved my hand around in the air and stirred my tormenters, but they wouldn't go away. It seemed that for every one that left, a dozen took his place. But I gained one thing. I knew Tucker couldn't, or didn't, see me move. If he had, I would have been dead.

Taking advantage of my new knowledge, I slipped the bandana from my neck and tied it around my head. It covered the wound and eased my mind, though there was plenty of sweat and blood to keep the feast going

183

on around my face. At least they couldn't get inside my head. It seemed important.

Not knowin', I can't say whether the flies tormentin' me kept my mind off the passin' of time and made it seem faster, or if their aggravation worked at me and made the time creep by. Maybe both. The minutes stretched endless. No breath of air moved save that stirred by the constant buzz of the fly's wings. Sweat ran down my face and soaked my shirt. And then it was dark.

I must have dozed off to have missed the setting of the sun. Out there, the sunset is not a thing to pass unnoticed even by the most calloused eye. It never sets quietly in a dignified promise to return another day. No, sir. The sun fights settin' like a man fights dyin' in the west. Just when it seems it's about to give it all up, it explodes into a flamin' blaze of glory as wide as the sky. A thousand colored streamers stretch out across the blue like giant fingers tryin' to grasp onto something to keep the sun from slippin' away. And when all is lost it defiantly shouts its oath to return in a single burst of brilliance, like a Mexican general shakin' his fist at a deposing army.

The sweat turned cold on my body. Not from the coolin' of the day, but from the knowin' how close to death I had been, and might still be.

The land was an unforgiving land. It had little patience with mistakes. A single mistake could bring a sudden end to all of man's problems. Already I had made more than most men were allowed in a lifetime in a single day. Less than a day. Only a few hours had passed since my day-dreaming had allowed Tucker to catch me unaware and throw me into such a desperate situation. I whispered a little prayer for bein' watched over in my stupidity. You never could tell. Preacher might be right. Anyway, it couldn't hurt.

My ears strained for a whisper of cloth pulled across the grasping thorns of mesquite bush, or the roll of a stone or snap of a twig under foot. There was nothing. Nothing but the night sounds of crickets and coyotes. And somewhere, way off, the hooting of an owl calling to his mate, and the pleading *Maaaaa* of a dogie calf calling for a mother that would never return.

My eyes penetrated the darkness far enough to keep me on edge. Every bush seemed to move when I wasn't watching, but never moved, even the gentle swaying in a breeze, while I watched.

I had always prided myself on bein' a patient man. Many times I laid on bare ground and waited out attacking Indians until their patience broke and carelessness made them easy victums for my guns. But as the night wore on, I began to feel like a fool. "If Tucker was still out there, he would have made a move by now," I told myself. "Hang in a little longer," I argued. "It ain't goin' to make any difference. If he's gone you can't catch him now." But I couldn't keep my mind off Annie and the others. It was mostly Annie I worried about.

If Tucker had abandoned me to go looking for the others, he was bitin' off more than he could chew. I knew Estavan's stalking skill. I've watched him sneak up to grabbin' distance of the sharp-eyed prong-horn antelope on the Llano. And I've seen him surprise a Comanche war party by bein' where they knew he wasn't. Estavan would have little trouble with Tucker. And Preacher not much more. He lacked Estavan's skills in the wild, but he had a will to live that had allowed him to take a dozen outlaw bullets into his body and be back in the saddle in little more than a week. It would take more than Tucker or even half a dozen Tuckers to handle that pair.

But Annie was a different matter. She was a child

of her parents' old age and they were gone on. She lived alone with her brother on the Baxter Ranch. The land was good and would someday support dozens of hired hands and great herds of cattle, but not yet. Only Joe Baxter stood between Tucker and Annie.

Joe was comin', but he wasn't yet a match for Tucker. Give him another year or two to harden in the ways of the land and he would be more than a match for whatever he faced. There wasn't a year or two to give. If Tucker had gone after the Baxters, they were as good as dead.

It tore at me. When a man takes on the responsibility for others, he becomes vulnerable to attacks from all sides. A few weeks before that, I could have waited Tucker out if it took days. But no longer. I couldn't ignore the chance that he had pulled out and left me hidin' in the brush while he went to murder Annie. I had to know.

I picked up a rock as big as my fist and heaved it as far as I could. Nothing. Either he was gone or he wasn't buying my decoy. But that didn't prove anything. The trick was so old not many greenhorns would have bought it. It was the best I had though, so I tried again. This time I threw a little stick into the brush just fifteen or twenty feet to my right. It sounded a whole lot more like the noise a man might make tryin' to move around in the thickets. But not enough to fool Tucker. If he was there.

I was plumb out of tricks and plumb out of patience. I decided it was time to lay my cards on the table. I might lose everything in one bad gamble, but a man can't set forever. Sooner or later he has to stand and be counted. At least those were the things I was tellin' myself in excuse for losing' patience. Actually it was more of a change of tactics than a loss of patience. I reasoned that Tucker had at least a good idea of where

I was. And he had the skill to stalk me. If I waited him out, I decided, he would have all the advantage.But if I could upset his plans, I might turn the advantage to myself. I was better than most with my gun and knew I could take him, if we met head on. It was to try to arrange such a meeting that I stepped out of the brush.

Like the politicians say, we had a quorum. I mean we were both there and the countin' of votes had started.

The blast from the fifty-caliber Sharps came from twenty feet away. The muzzle blast lit the space like a candle, only real quick, then gone. I would have recognized the blast of the big bore anywhere. The Sharps had a bark like no other gun. But I didn't have to count on recognizing the sound. I knew the gun. It was the same rifle I took from Sam's wagon and gave to Tucker out on the Llano. I made quite a to-do about a man shouldn't go unarmed in such a hostile land. I didn't know the man was more hostile than the land.

My movement must have taken Tucker completely by surprise. That's the only way I figure he could have missed at such close range. That and the fact that he fired before I got completely straightened up. Half a second later the shot would have taken my head off.

I answered with three shots from the Patterson as fast as I could thumb the hammer, one to the right and one to the left of the muzzle flash. The third shot I placed into the ground where I figured Tucker dropped. He was hit. No man could fake the agony in that scream. The question was, how hard? It could be anything from a flesh wound to a heart shot.

My Patterson Colt carried a five-shot cylinder. I squeezed off the other two shots followin' the one that

more than my share of mistukes with Tucker. I re-
charged my pistol and capped it off before I went for
a closer look. "It's funny!" I said to the body. "Half
a dozen times I slipped up and got away with it. But
one mistake was too many for you." Maybe there's
more to Preacher's ideas than I thought, I said to myself.

I would have pondered it more but the sun was
coming up and there were miles between Annie and
me.

THE OTHER SIDE OF THE CANYON

ROMER ZANE GREY

THE OTHER SIDE OF THE CANYON marks the return to print of one of Zane Grey's strongest characters, Laramie Nelson, first introduced in Grey's novel RAIDERS OF SPANISH PEAKS. Laramie was a seasoned Indian fighter, an incomparable tracker, and one of the deadliest gunhands the West had ever known.

In these stories, Romer Zane Grey, son of the master storyteller, continues Laramie's adventures as he takes on a gang of train robbers, a gold thief, and a sharp-shooting woman wanted for murder!

WESTERN
0-8439
2041-6
$2.75

THE RIDER OF DISTANT TRAILS

ROMER ZANE GREY

The Rider Of Distant Trails marks the return to print of one of Zane Grey's most memorable characters, Buck Duane, first introduced in Grey's novel *Lone Star Ranger*. Forced to turn outlaw as a young man, Buck later teamed up with Captain Jim MacNelly of the Texas Rangers and proved himself to be the Ranger's deadliest gun.

In these stories, Romer Zane Grey, son of the master storyteller, continues Buck's adventures in Texas and as he takes on outlaws who are terrorizing ranches and towns in this tough cattle country!

WESTERN
0-8439-2082-3
$2.75